D0640941

How Green Was My Apple

How Green Was My Apple

MARC LOVELL

PUBLISHED FOR THE CRIME CLUB BY
DOUBLEDAY & COMPANY, INC.
GARDEN CITY, NEW YORK
1984

All of the characters in this book
are fictitious, and any resemblance
to actual persons, living or dead,
is purely coincidental.

Library of Congress Cataloging in Publication Data

Lovell, Marc.
How green was my apple.

I. Title.
PR6062.O853H6   1984   823'.914

ISBN 0-385-19107-3
Library of Congress Catalog Card Number 83–14106
Copyright © 1984 by Doubleday & Company, Inc.
All Rights Reserved
Printed in the United States of America
First Edition

How Green Was My Apple

CHAPTER 1

The United Kingdom Philological Institute had its home in an elegant mansion in Kensington. The basement, formerly the below-stairs world of servants, was nowadays an assembly hall. It was used for conferences and classes, lectures and film shows, as well as the staff Christmas parties which no one talked about afterwards, even in medieval French.

Present this Friday afternoon in the hall were thirty young Norwegians, male and female. Advanced students of English, they gave close attention to today's speaker, the tall man called Appleton Porter, who was talking about British Personality and Character. Their expressions seemed to suggest not so much scientific interest as sympathy.

Apple looked at his watch. It was the third time he had done this, and he told himself that if he did it again he would get annoyed. A show of impatience was ill-mannered.

"In conclusion," Apple said. "I should like to say a few words on the subject of English eccentricity. I have my own theory on the puzzling trait, which, incidentally, is peculiar to the middle and upper classes. No labourer was ever eccentric. His only concern with history is in its personal and recent form—when Dad lost his job in the thirties and so forth."

From outdoors came the beep of a car horn. Apple, not looking at his watch, went on:

"The English eccentric is afraid and insecure. All island peoples are, of course, which is why they take so readily to excess gambling and drinking. But in the Englishman this is exaggerated by the fact that he shares his island with two other races, the Scots and the Welsh, while another race, the Irish, is right next door, and with a dozen more a few miles away on the Continent."

Apple tapped the lectern with a polite forefinger. "All throughout history, therefore, the English establishment has needed to be on its guard. Defence takes various forms. One is to lull possible enemies into a sense of security. So the eccentric unconsciously acts out, *I am a fool. I am likeable and quite harmless. Few of my eccentricities are ever dangerous or offensive. Generally, in fact, they're charming. Have no fear of me.*

"From insecurity, then, comes the desire to create security, in others. If the complacent enemy attacks, he will expect vapid, muddle-headed, disorganised resistance. He will be totally unprepared for the brilliance and ferocity of the defence."

Picking up his notes, Apple shoved them in a pocket of his sober grey suit. "That is all, ladies and gentlemen. Thank you for your attention. Good afternoon."

Quickly, before anyone could ask a question, Apple left the lectern and strode off the low platform. At the hall's side he ignored a lift on account of his claustrophobia and pushed through swing doors. With long-legged ease he took the stairs three at a time.

Appleton Porter was good-looking in the way that's never noticed because it's a standard. He had attractive green eyes that appeared to be vaguely worried. His sandy hair was as boring to him in colour as it was in short-cut neatness, though less of a nuisance than his complexion. Apple's face was pale behind the freckles which were spread about with a discouraging lack of pattern. But he no longer worried over his looks, he told himself regularly.

On an upper floor of the building, Apple went along a passage to a door that was slightly larger than the others. He knocked, checked his watch, went in at a call of:

"Please—um—"

The office was untidy, a spinster's nightmare, with a large desk forming the core of the mess. The light fog came from two pipes; one, forgotten, smouldered in an ashtray, another was in Professor Warden's mouth.

The old man came around his desk. He was small and thin, with white hair that matched his old-fashioned suit. His manner was bewildered, like that of a lost tracker dog. Although the professor spoke fourteen languages fluently, he often had trouble finding the word he wanted in English.

"Afternoon, my boy."

"Good afternoon, sir," Apple said. He stood holding the door open for the fresh air.

Professor Warden had kept moving, circling. He finished up back at his chair. Sitting, he took the pipe out of his mouth and said, "I'm worried about Romansh."

"Romance, professor?"

"The language, my boy, not the condition." He blinked through smoke. "Curious case of mis-hearing, that. You haven't done it again, have you? Fallen in—er —?"

"Love?"

"Yes."

"No."

"What a relief. It makes you a trifle abstracted, I always think."

Apple looked at his watch. "I'm sorry, sir."

"But to Romansh," Professor Warden said. "Which, as you are aware, is Switzerland's fourth official language, following French, German and Italian. It's spoken by only a handful of people."

"Thirty-seven thousand, actually," Apple said. Apple

was an infomaniac, a collector of oddities of data, ninety-five percent of which were useless. "Most of the people live in a remote canton."

"It's an ancient hybrid of Latin," the old man said, "widely accepted to have been founded when the Romans conquered the mountain region about two thousand years ago."

"Fifteen B.C., I believe, sir."

"But the point is, Porter, what are we going to do about it?" He waved his pipe like a sword.

"Do, professor?"

"Romansh is on the verge of—um—er—"

"Discovery?"

"No, Porter, not at all. The verge of—ah—"

Anxiously, Apple suggested, "Death? Revival? Defeat?"

The old man said, "That's it, my boy. Death. Romansh is going the way of Cornish and Manx and many others. And we have to *do* something before it's too late."

Apple looked at his watch. "Yes, professor, I agree one hundred percent. But what I came to see you about was time. To ask, in fact, if I could leave a little early for the weekend."

"On Friday, you mean?"

"It's Friday now, sir. And I'd like to leave at once, if that's all right with you."

"My dear boy," Professor Warden said, smiling, "as a senior offical here at the United Kingdom Philological Institute, you are certainly entitled to a little leeway in the matter of working hours. Therefore the answer to your question is in the affirmative."

"Thank you, professor."

"There was no real need to ask it in the first place."

"Thank you," Apple said, retreating through the doorway. "Good afternoon."

Reaching his free hand towards the pipe in the ashtray, the old man said absently, "I appreciate your advice."

Apple closed the door. As he turned and walked along the corridor, he warned himself not to take on as a worry the possible extinction of Romansh.

Around a corner came a pretty secretary. Apple, his mind on the lecture he had just given and its relation to Professor Warden, sagged automatically at the knees while passing the girl and mused that life must be difficult for people who were eccentric.

Apple came out onto the front steps of the Institute. On the roadway traffic was brisk, as always, but on the pavement pedestrians moved slowly in the mildness and sunshine that were unexpected gifts in early March.

Apple went down the steps. At the bottom he was brought to a stop by a woman who moved out of the stream of passers-by. She raised a gloved finger and said, "Excuse me."

Apple put a hand over his watch. "Yes, ma'am?"

"I do hope you don't mind me approaching you like this."

"Not in the least."

About fifty years old, the woman wore suburbia's uniform: neat coat, sensible shoes, gloves, small hat. Her blue rinse was suitably pale, her cosmetics hardly detectable. She had quick brown foxy eyes.

Her voice drawling lazily, she said, "If one may ask, how tall are you?"

"Six feet seven inches," Apple said. He gave a smile of apology.

"In your socks?"

"In my bare feet."

"Good heavens," the woman said.

Apple wondered with discomfort if it was proper to use the word "bare" to this type of woman, a thought he then swiftly amended to cover women of all types. Yes, he decided. In this day and age, of course.

"But the gist is," the woman said, "what does your height have to do with languages?"

As Apple fumbled for an answer, the woman went on in her drawl to tell of the hundreds of times she had passed the Institute, had been curious as to what exactly went on there, had never thought to enquire until seeing this terribly tall chap come sweeping out.

Keeping a hand over his watch, source of his impatience, Apple listened. He stood bent from the hips. It gave him an ache in the small of the back. But over the years he had tried all the height-reducing stances, and this one was best. If he held himself upright and with his head lowered, he got a pain in the neck; if he held his head as upright as his body, his downcast eyes took on a sinister appearance; if he adopted a sideways lean, he looked broken. Apple, therefore, always bent, even though he knew the pose had a hint of condescension.

The woman said, "So do tell me, please, young man, what you actually do in this place."

With an inner sigh, Apple began to explain. It bored him. To compensate, he told about the other side of the coin, but kept it in his head: "My work here is part cover. Even Professor Warden doesn't know that I'm an operative with British Intelligence. I have been since leaving university, where I was enrolled because of my languages. I speak six fluently and a dozen others with competence but an accent. For the Service I do translations, read and write letters, sit in as interpretor on high-level international conferences. Obviously, I have a 10 rating in security."

Apple left his imagined discourse there. He didn't go on to admit that he was rarely used in any other capacity —as, for example, an agent in the field. The rest of his ratings were feeble, for one thing (unarmed combat 6,

lying ability 6, resistance to pain 5, interest in gossip 4).
For another thing, he was far too tall for the necessary
dimming of physical presence. A third reason was his low
tolerance for alcohol, while a truly damning fourth was
the fact that he had a sympathetic nature, so would find
it difficult to be ruthless if such was needed. Those few
times when his Control, Angus Watkin, had used him as
an operative on a mission, he had failed to be brilliant.

Apple finished his description of endeavours at the
United Kingdom Philological Institute. As expected, the
woman looked unimpressed.

She drawled, "I see, young man. That's terribly interesting."

"It is rather, yes."

She glanced at her watch. "Sorry, but I must be off."

"Excuse me for rambling on," Apple said. "Good afternoon."

"Good-bye."

Striding away with a relieved squaring of his shoulders, Apple reflected that it would be nice to be able to
tell someone that he worked for Intelligence. He had
never breathed it to a soul, though he had been strongly
tempted with two or three special girlfriends, not as an
image booster but as evidence of his undying love. Now
Apple tried to remember those girls' names.

Two minutes later, turning a corner, he thought:
Ethel. She had come into view, was there waiting where
he had left her. He stopped for a moment to gaze upon
her with pride and devotion.

Ethel was a London taxi. For three decades she had
been in government service, in undercover operations
with Vice, Customs & Excise, Narcotics, branches of the
regular police, and, in her final years, with the various
departments of Intelligence.

At last, Ethel had been declared redundant. Not only
was her old-fashioned squareness an anomaly, but she

had become known to every spy in the Western theatre of operations. The government had put her on sale in a public auction. Apple, shocked by the callousness of it all, had later bought her from the highest bidder.

For a while he had kept Ethel exactly as she was—except for a tune-up and new rubber. It became a nuisance, however, being hailed by cab seekers and then sometimes cursed for not stopping. Apple had taken Ethel to the best coachwork firm in London.

Although physically unchanged—hire sign and meter still there—the old taxi had lost her lifetime black. She was now painted pale green, with an orange stripe around the middle, and red wheels. Ethel was bright, startling, outrageous. Apple didn't know where he had found the courage.

Nor did he know, even faintly, that Ethel's facade formed the answer in part to his yearning to express the rebel who lived restlessly inside him; that swinger who fought against the sentimentality, the conformity, the neat hair and dull ties and suits of super drabness. All Apple did know was that when he sat at the steering wheel he felt singularly contented.

He went on across the street. Noticing, with an enjoyable frown, a speck of grease on the chrome radiator, he brought from his breast pocket a perfectly folded handkerchief. With it he stroked the grease into oblivion. He refolded the handkerchief with the blemish inside and returned it to its place.

Apple got in the driver's seat. As he did so, his movements had a hint of ceremony. He pretended, even to himself, that he wasn't aware of the small boy who stood staring as if at a regiment of hussars.

The engine hummed to life at a touch of the starter. Apple slotted first gear into place, released the hand brake and took Ethel away from the kerb. Slowly, as he drove, his face grew a faint, dreamy smile.

Because of getting away before the rush-hour traffic began, Apple had left London behind within half an hour. He bowled along a quiet road at five miles under the legal limit. He wasn't going to allow his eagerness to tempt him into breaking the law.

Apple's goal was his country cottage. He used it on weekends, both as a sanctuary and a love nest. In recent months its main value had been in relation to Monico.

There being a no-pets rule in Apple's apartment house, he had needed to sneak his dog in and out for exercise and nature calls and keep him cooped up indoors throughout the day, giving him total freedom only from Friday to Monday.

Tiring at last of the excitement afforded by his covert activities, no longer warmed by his blatant rule violation, Apple had made a board-and-keep arrangement with a farmer.

This past week had been Monico's first as a boarder. Apple had missed his welcomes and presence at the flat. He was eager to see his dog, also to learn how the arrangement was working. He had reservations about the farmer, who referred to Monico as "this here animal of yours."

Apple whistled as he drove. The countryside was pretty, leafing out into spring. Birds swooped playfully ahead of Ethel, whom Apple treated with respect for her age on hills. When he reached the midway point between cottage and London, he whistled a more jaunty air and slightly slackened the knot of his tie.

Apple came into a village. It was a one-donkey straggle of houses, post office, pub. More often than not, Apple had a drink here to break the journey. But not today.

He was almost through the village when a policeman appeared, suddenly, like a stage villain bounding out from the wings. The stripeless constable, young and thin, stepped off the kerb with one arm rigidly raised.

Braking, Apple almost frowned. Three delays in a row, he thought: Professor Warden, the woman and now a copper. Would this be the clincher, third time unlucky?

With Ethel stopped, the constable came to the window. Apple told him as pleasantly as he could that he had been doing only twenty-eight miles an hour.

"Spot check," the policeman said, stern, hiding buck teeth. He looked nearly old enough to vote. "I would like to see, please, your driving licence, your insurance, and your Ministry of Transport certificate of roadworthiness."

Apple handed out a wallet of car papers. "I'm in a bit of a hurry, officer."

"They all say that."

"Do they really?"

The constable flicked a glimpse of his teeth. "Makes you wonder what they've been up to."

Apple laughed guiltily. He said, "I've just come from work."

"They could've robbed a bank. Anything."

"Straight from work without stopping anywhere."

"Yes, sir," the policeman said. He began, slowly, to look at the papers.

Wearing a false smile, Apple sat in a slump to signify lack of hurry. He had his fingers and feet taut to counter unconscious drumming or tapping. From the corners of his eyes he watched with impatience the constable's plod through the wallet and, with curiosity, his frequent glances back along the road.

Finally seeming to be satisfied, though still holding on to the documents, the constable asked, "Where's the rest of 'em?"

"The rest of what?"

"The vehicles. The others of your circus."

Apple shook his head. "I'm not with a circus, officer." He reached a hand towards his wallet. "Well, if that's all."

Putting both hands behind his back, the policeman said as though musing aloud, "This here vehicle."

"It's being used to try out various types and colours of paint. How they stand up to pollution and the weather."

"You're not with a circus?"

"I'm not, no. Sorry."

"Oh well."

"If I could have my papers back, please."

After glancing along the road, the constable said, again musingly, "This hurry of yours."

"It's nothing desperate, officer," Apple said in a winning way. "But I would like to get on. I'm seeing someone special this weekend." He gave a lascivious wink.

To Apple's surprise and alarm and instant compassion, the constable started to blush. A pinkness crept up out of his uniform collar to coat his neck and face like a rapid case of fever. Apple, himself a *grand mal* blusher, absently gave the policeman's attack a 7.

As Apple knew only too well, diversion was all-important, along with lack of audience. Therefore, while looking in the other direction, he began to talk quickly, describing a short-term cure for blushing. It was one of the many he had used over the years, all bought through advertisements in magazines, all ultimately becoming inefficacious through familiarity. That he didn't offer the latest cure was because he hadn't tried it himself yet.

"What you do is imagine yourself in a snowdrift," Apple said in the necessary conversational tone. "You're lying there and you can't get up. The idea of the danger and the cold does the trick, if your attack isn't too severe. If it's a bad one, you see yourself as dead. If it's . . ."

Sensing a change in the setting, Apple broke off and

looked the other way. The constable was nowhere to be seen. Apple twisted around in his seat.

Behind, a car was coming to a stop near where the young policeman stood—stood almost at attention. The car was plain black. Its driver, sole occupant, was a plump man of early middle age. He had a vicious scar on one cheek.

Apple felt a twinge of excitement.

Halting his car, the driver got out and went around to the constable, who saluted. They talked briefly. After another salute, the policeman came striding back. Without a word he handed the wallet through the window, passed on and went from sight around a corner.

Next came the scar-faced man. He opened the rear door, got in, slid back the glass panel and said, casually, "Hello, Apple."

"Hi, Bill."

"Let's get this carnival rolling, eh?"

"Of course," Apple said, with difficulty aping the other man's casual manner. "At your service."

In spookspeak, the cant of the espionage business, Appleton Porter was one of the faceless ones. These were people with a specialty. In Apple's case it was languages. With others it might be the gift of water divining, a knowledge of botany or the ability to milk venom out of snakes. Faceless ones were used seldom.

At the top end of the spy scale were field operatives, those men and women who risked their health, sanity and lives in playing out the games which had been devised by Upstairs—spookspeak for the higher reaches of Intelligence.

Between the two personnel extremes came people like Bill Burton. Since a scar which had been caused in childhood made his face memorable, Burton could never be an agent in the field, though he sometimes acted as backup man on missions. Generally he did courier work, driving or tailing or guarding jobs, initial interrogations and burglaries. He was an all-rounder.

Because of the need-to-know principle, Apple had met few of his colleagues. Only his chief, Angus Watkin, had he seen more often than Bill Burton. He knew that Bill was married, a non-drinker, a crack shot with a revolver and the possessor of two or three languages, but he didn't know where he lived or if Bill Burton was his real name.

Driving on after steering into the road indicated by his passenger, Apple turned his head to the side. "Who did that copper think you were?"

"A god from Scotland Yard," Bill Burton said. "We used his name in vain to have you stopped."

"All comes clear."

"You caused us a bit of strife, old son. You usually go straight home from work."

Apple explained while getting out cigarettes. He and Bill Burton lit up. Apple said, as Burton went back to lounge on the seat, "Use the ashtray, please."

"Naturally. Good old Eth. She's looking great."

"Thank you."

"Must be thirty-five if she's a day."

"Thirty-one," Apple said in a snap.

"Did you hear about the time she . . ."

Despite knowing the anecdote, and despite his simmer of excitement, Apple listened carefully. He was sorry when the story ended. Although tempted to tell one of his own, the simmer made him ask, "So where're we going?"

"To a boozer. Be there in five minutes."

"And what's this all about?"

Bill Burton grinned at Apple via the rear-view mirror. "Ask me no questions, as the saying starts to go."

Which was an ironical joke, Apple knew. An agent

would lie to his nearest and dearest. It was in the blood
that had been transfused steadily since early training
days.

Apropos of lying and an earlier thought, Apple wondered if Bill Burton had told his wife that he worked for
Intelligence. But he realised at once that he already had
the answer, that if he were less of an amateur in the spy
game he would never have pondered the question.

Bill's wife did not, of course, know what her husband
did for a living. All agents stayed behind the cloak in
respect of spouses and kin. Like need-to-know and the
cell system, it was a matter of protection that worked
both ways. No family member could give away or have
extracted from him information which he didn't possess.
The silence was observed by all espionage organisations,
and known to be, so no agent's family and associates
were ever bothered by the opposition.

Apple didn't go on to think about torture. He didn't
believe it actually happened, for one thing. For another,
the suggestion of gross brutality would interfere with his
romantic view of all that was connected with spying.

Shuddering over what he didn't believe happened,
not for a moment, Apple took a final drag on his cigarette. He put it out in the gleaming ashtray and said, "All
right, Bill, no questions."

"I'm only bragging by inference anyway," the scar-
faced man said. "I don't know a bloody thing."

"That's always possible."

"Course it is. Would you and I ever be anything but
perfectly straight with each other?"

In physical and verbal unison, both men shook their
heads and chanted musically, "No, no, no."

The pub stood in open country. It was ringed by tow-
ering yew trees, fronted by a horse trough that held
potted plants and sided by an extensive parking area.

Opening time being only minutes past, the park had but one car. It was plain grey.

Apple brought Ethel to a stop under a tree. As he got out, into a trill of birdsong, he noted that behind the pub was a bowling green. On the immaculate, carpetlike sward a lone figure was at practice, rolling brown wooden balls towards the small white jack.

Apple closed his door quietly. After doing the same, Bill Burton said, "Off you go, old son. See you."

Nodding, Apple moved away. Even if he hadn't been excited, he still wouldn't have bothered to ask how Burton was going to get back to his car; that would have been arranged. Apple headed for the bowler.

Angus Watkin was a plain-brown-wrapper of a man. From the crown of his averagely neat brown hair to the soles of his medium-clean brown shoes, he was plain, bland, unnoticeable. His suit and tie were like a million others. Save for the heavy-lidded eyes, his face would have defeated anyone who was bent on giving a description. He could have passed as a carpenter or a lawyer, a major on leave or a fading pimp. He looked about fifty years old and not particularly intelligent; looked no more like a spymaster than Apple looked like a dwarf.

His tall underling, approaching from behind, halted nearby on the grass and cleared his throat. Angus Watkin went on watching the ball he had just released and stayed in his bowling stoop. The ball trickled to a stop— three inches from the jack. Watkin slowly straightened and slowly turned.

"Stupid game, bowls," he said in his colourless voice. "Don't you agree, Porter?"

Apple said, "Yes, sir." He knew nothing about the game but at this moment he would have agreed that his ears ought to be amputated.

Angus Watkin murmured, "Acquiescence." It sounded like an admonition.

Apple cleared his throat again. He reminded himself, as he had many times in the past, that there was probably a solid reason why his Control always behaved in such a hateful manner, which somehow failed to make Apple dislike the man any the less.

"As you will possibly have gathered by now," Watkin said, "I have a little errand for you." That was spook-speak for mission, and the only slang Watkin ever used.

Apple allowed his excitement to rise from simmer to boil. He stood straight, bent again and said an alert, cool "Very good, sir."

"It starts almost at once and I trust therefore that your services are available." Only the words were sarcastic, not the tone.

"They are, sir, yes."

Angus Watkin said, "This is a two-man operation, Porter. You will have a partner."

Apple asked, "Would that be Bill Burton?" He winced at his mistake: Watkin didn't like correct forecasts. But the question turned out right, being wrong.

"No it would not," the older man said. "Your partner, in point of fact, is female."

Apple bent an inch or two lower. "That's interesting."

"Is it? Then I suppose I had better remind you of the business-only rule."

"I know it, sir. No fraternising, on or off the job."

"Quite so," Angus Watkin said. He gazed around casually, as if counting the bowling green's edging of benches, each separated from the next by a table. "You will be meeting the lady shortly, but I can fill you in on a few details."

"Thank you, sir. It's best to be prepared."

Watkin gave one of his sighs. He said, "She will be known to you as Kate. You will be known to her as Basil. There are no number-names in this operation. Its comparative insignificance doesn't warrant such."

"Oh," Apple said. His boil calmed.

"Kate is a professional. She has been on dozens of missions. As a matter of fact, her father was also in the Service. She knows the trade backwards."

A female Watkin, Apple thought with a return to simmer. But it would be useful, an education, to work with an old campaigner, a real pro.

His Control went on, "For some reason, however, the lady is somewhat prickly on the subject of her background. Perhaps the prima-donna syndrome, perhaps modesty, perhaps one of those female quirks. Who knows?" His lips twitched, which was a smile. It said that the idea of Angus Watkin not being cognizant of every facet of his underlings' lives was hilarious.

"Who indeed, sir?"

"Therefore, Porter, the subject should not be raised. You will treat Kate, in fine, as though she were on your own level."

Apple stood his full height. You putrid old biblical-senser, he thought while saying that he understood perfectly, he wouldn't breathe a word.

Angus Watkin gestured to the side in excessive politeness. "Shall we sit down?" He strolled away.

Following, Apple saw that on one of the tables were two glasses. He could tell what they contained: Scotch and water for his Control, and for himself sherry on the rocks, which was his favourite drink.

While Angus Watkin knew most everything about Appleton Porter, Apple was aware, including the name of his dog, Appleton Porter knew nothing whatever about Angus Watkin. But in times of high dislike, such as now, Apple enjoyed giving his chief a background.

He lives in a dreary suburb. His house is small, with next door a drunken couple and six screechy kids, with above the flightpath of Heathrow, with across the narrow street a twenty-four-hour petrol station. His large wife has muscles and a moustache and a loud snore. She cooks like a Boy Scout. She eats garlic for her constant cough, cabbage for her flatulence. She has a mother.

It helped. Mentally humming, Apple sat on the bench at his drink's side of the table. Watkin had sat at the other side. They lifted their glasses and sipped.

Apple asked permission to smoke. After a nod to signal assent, a sniff to show disapproval and a tutting sound to express regret at the addiction, Angus Watkin said, "To your errand. It concerns someone here in Britain, in London, although he is a citizen of the Soyuz Sovetskikh Sotsialisticheskikh Respublik." He was not above show-ing off, when his mood was good. "The gentleman's name is Alexander Grishin. Sound familiar?"

Resisting a bluff, Apple said, "No, sir."

"Of course not. Grishin is a nobody. He doesn't even reside at number fifteen Kensington Palace Gardens."

"Thirteen," Apple corrected quietly, as was expected of him. "The Soviet Embassy."

His chief, who had hardly paused, continued blithely, "Our man Alexander Grishin lives at one of the Em-bassy's overflow houses. It's about a third of a mile away, west, just off Holland Park Avenue. Know the place, Porter?"

Lighting a cigarette, Apple nodded. He said, "It's in Oranger Lane."

"Grishin's job at the Embassy is as part of the mainte-nance staff. He's been there for three years. Only re-cently has he come to my notice, by which I mean has he not acted true to form. I suspect that he's up to some-thing. If he is, I would like to find out what."

"Naturally, sir."

"So you, Porter, working with agent Kate, will keep a watch on the gentleman, starting in about two hours from now, when we have a firm on his intended move-ments."

"Very good, sir. Thank you."

As though absently, Angus Watkin said, "I'm a little shorthanded at the moment."

"Ah."

"You will watch the gentleman from a distance, not get involved. Nor will you go sidetracking. Clear?"

"Perfectly, sir."

Watkin slid a piece of paper across the table. "That's where and how you will meet Kate. Go straight there from here. No, Porter, don't read it now."

Apple put the paper in his pocket. "A question, sir?"

"No. Anything else you need will be supplied by Kate, who, by the by, will be at the rendezvous on time. Finish your odd concoction, Porter."

Enjoying neither drink nor cigarette, Apple sipped and smoked. He was eager to leave. It was a combination of a desire to get started on the mission and a lust to escape from his chief's presence.

Angus Watkin, one of whose pet hates was Naval Intelligence, began to talk lazily about Sir Francis Drake and his juvenile infatuation with the game of bowls.

Apple asked his question of himself: If this was a simple I-spy operation, what was the need for urgency—as suggested by an immediate start and the elaborations used to get hold of Appleton Porter? Why couldn't it have waited till Monday?

Dusk was beginning by the time Apple reached the vicinity of Euston Station and found a parking slot. Lights were twinkling on as if aware of his excitement. He got out and locked Ethel's doors.

Two youths ambled up. They had punk-jagged hair and wore unkempt uniforms that resembled those of the French Foreign Legion.

"All right, mate," one youth said. "We'll have a couple of vanillas."

Having been through this before, Apple was unruffled. He said, "This isn't an ice-cream cart."

The other youth snorted, "You trying to be funny or something?"

"Come on, mate. Two vanillas. We ain't got all day."

Pocketing his keys, Apple said, "Sold out. Sorry."

"Strawberry, then. We're easy to get along with."

"Then get along with ease," Apple said. He smiled at his wit as he strode away.

Raucously, the youths called after him that he was a short-arsed pimp and that their money was as good as the next thief's.

Apple put them out of his mind almost at once. He was thinking Instructions. The piece of paper given to him by Angus Watkin he had stopped on the way here to read and then burn.

That Instructions had been given in writing rather than verbally, Apple assumed, was on account of their spy-typical quality. For that same reason Watkin hadn't wanted them read in his presence. He had no sense of the picturesque, only of the convoluted.

Kate would be somewhere on the concourse of Euston Station. Approach was to be left to her. She would be carrying a small blue hold-all that bore the initials TWA, plus—for the usual secondary feature—a rolled copy of the *Daily Worker.*

Contact Signals were: Could you direct me to the lost-property office, please?/Sorry, miss, I'm a stranger here myself./It's a green umbrella./I hope you find it.

The Scrub Signal was: I've missed my train.

Apple had it down pat. He could, in fact, have quoted it backwards if necessary.

The concourse of the new railway station was crowded and bustly. At any other time Apple would have reflected with regret on the passing of the old Euston, with its vaulting roof and satanic smell of sulphur. Now he didn't give it a thought.

Hands afted, Apple wandered through the crowd. He hoped he gave the impression of being here to meet an arrival, perhaps an old uncle who worked on various charities.

Apple came to a pleased halt, the mission taking a step backwards in his mind, when he noticed a tall girl. She towered head and shoulders above the people near the huge departure board, at which she was looking. In her mid-twenties, she had long fair hair and a pretty face.

If it weren't for the operation he would approach the girl on some pretext, Apple assured himself, while knowing he didn't have the nerve to do any such thing. He sighed and strolled on.

There were many lone women, but those who gave Apple more than passing attention did so because of his height, he could tell. The crowd eddied, greeters shrieked, the late ran in panic. As if directing the way to the bedroom, a female voice breathed via loudspeakers that the train now standing at platform . . .

Close at hand, another female voice said, "Excuse me."

Apple stopped and turned. Standing there was the tall girl he had seen a minute ago. The startled thought came to him that she was doing what he lacked the nerve for. Then he was startled in a different direction.

The girl asked, "Could you direct me to the lost-property office, please?"

Apple stared. He collected himself with a jerk and said, "No." His face twitched. "I mean: Sorry, miss, I'm a stranger here myself."

"It's a green umbrella."

"I hope you find it."

The girl nodded, smiling faintly. She wore jeans and a

sweater, carried the correct features, one in either hand, and had on a pair of flat-heel shoes.

Apple was unable to prevent "You *are* tall."

"Yes, Basil," the girl said. "I'm six one."

You are also the owner of big blue eyes and a cute nose, Apple thought, settling. He said, "I'm six seven. Hello, Kate."

"Hello. It's nice not to want to sit down."

"I know exactly what you mean."

They smiled in mutual sympathy. Apple could hardly believe his luck. Not only was agent Kate wonderfully tall, she was attractive and a real pro to boot. He would have to watch his step.

"Um—how about a cup of tea, Kate?"

She said, "There isn't enough time. We start in an hour and I have to go to base first, to change."

"Where is it that we start?"

"Earl's Court. There's an exhibition on of inventions, gadgets. Our mark will be there." She handed over the rolled newspaper. "In that is a photo of him plus physical details. When you've absorbed . . ." She narrowed one eye.

Wishing he could do that, Apple said, "Right. Burn and flush. And we need each other's telephone numbers, don't we?"

They exchanged verbally. While Apple was absorbing through the customary tenfold repetition, he got a familiar sensation across his shoulders. Like a finger being trailed there, it meant he was being watched.

He asked, "Are we clean?"

"As far as I know, yes. At this stage of the game, we're sure to be, aren't we?"

"Yes, of course, of course." He told himself that, not unusually, the watcher could merely be someone staring at a man who was far taller than average. Or, equally standard, Angus Watkin could have detailed an agent to play observer-reporter.

Kate said, "You speak Russian, I understand, as well as about a thousand other languages."

"Well, a couple."

"I only have Russian and German. French I know but I avoid speaking it because my accent's so bloody awful."

Apple held back from saying that it was merely a matter of learning to half swallow the tongue. Kate could be exaggerating because of her modesty.

He said, "Russian's all we need for this caper, I imagine."

"Yes, but Alexander Grishin does know quite a bit of English. He's been here years, after all."

"Are we going to get close enough to him to use any language? That's not likely on an I-spy, is it?"

"Time will tell," Kate said, brushing a long strand of fair hair away from her face. "I haven't thought much about after tonight. Tomorrow, I suppose, we'll just pick him up when he leaves the residence and play it from there."

Apple asked, "What else do we have firm on our Alex?"

"I've given you everything that Mr. Watkin gave me. But that's not saying a lot."

Apple enjoyed the pro touch, the gentle derision of "Mr." He said, "Watkin wouldn't tell you the time if you were falling off Big Ben."

Kate's faint smile came on again. "Well, we agree on that. It's a good start."

"Couldn't be better."

She glanced over to the large clock. "I have to split. Shall we say eight, just inside the main entrance?"

A moment later Apple was alone, watching Kate move majestically away through the crowd. He realised two factors. One, the finger-tickle sensation was no longer there on his back. Two, he was deeply smitten.

The apartment in Harlequin Mansions, Bloomsbury, began with a passage. Off it opened the various rooms, all of which were of ample proportions. The height of the old-fashioned doorways appealed particularly to its tenant. Never once since living here had he made that instinctive, unconscious, fractional ducking motion which was a part of his life elsewhere.

After Apple opened the door to his flat, the first thing that came into his head was Monico. He had been reminded by the lack of that tumultuous welcome which he still missed even after a week. What next came into his head was the shameful fact that not once had he thought of his dog since being stopped by the policeman.

Slamming the door, switching on lights, Apple hurried into his living room, to the telephone on a corner table near the fireplace. He dialled a number with hard jabs and flicked twirls. When Farmer Galling answered, Apple splurged into an excuse based on sudden illness. He concluded: "So I won't be able to make it down there this weekend. Would you please explain that to Monico."

After silence came a hollow-sounding, "You want me to explain . . ."

"Well, perhaps not the whole thing. Just say I'm unavoidably detained. I'll be there as soon as I can. Thank you, Mr. Galling. Good evening."

Feeling less traitorous, Apple hurried to the bathroom. As he showered, his excitement came back, first about the mission, last about Kate. He thought of her long hair and prettiness, recalled the thrust of her breasts under the sweater, remembered the sway of her shapely hips as she moved away. He turned the temperature dial to cold.

Towelling himself vigorously, Apple considered the

business aspect of his partner. He had been twinned with Kate, obviously, so that his height would draw attention away from her, make her look fairly average from a distance. Apple had to admit that it was a shrewd move on Angus Watkin's part, even though it stated clearly which of the twins was the more important, the real pro.

Dressed in flannels, blazer and a roll-neck sweater, Apple went to the living room. Before picking up the feature which had been handed to him by Kate, he closed the curtains for the spyness of it.

Flattened out and opened page by page, the newspaper gave up a passport-size photograph. On its reverse side were data in microscopic longhand. Alexander Grishin was of average build, aged forty-seven, wore lower dentures, had the nail missing from the little finger of his left hand.

The full-face picture—taken, Apple guessed, outdoors with a telescope lens—showed simian features and flat dark hair. The Russian was very Russian.

Apple burned the photograph and flushed the black crumble down the lavatory. Before leaving the flat, he paused by the hatstand behind the main door to look in its mirror and try narrowing one eye.

Apple trotted down three flights of carpeted stairs. Letting himself out, he strode directly across the street. Abruptly, in the centre of the roadway, he came to a halt.

Ahead, between a truck and a car, was an empty parking space. It was in that space that Apple had left Ethel.

Oncoming headlights and a horn blast sent him on. He stood in the emptiness and looked around. His heart was tapping at speed. That Ethel had been stolen he quickly dismissed: no thief in his right mind would take such an old and noticeable vehicle for profit.

Thief. The word triggered recollection of the two punks. Had they followed him home and taken Ethel out of spite? It was possible, but more probably she had been borrowed by kids bent on doing the joyride bit.

Apple's heart slowed, even though there was still damage to worry about. He thought over what action he should take.

Contacting the authorities was out. The last thing you did if you were in trouble while on a mission was go to the police. Apart from other complications, they might find out who you really were. Policemen were people. They talked. One of those who knew what you were might have a wife whose cousin had a brother-in-law whose psychiatrist went to a pub which had a barmaid whose nephew's girlfriend worked at the Hungarian Embassy. From such frail beginnings did many of the great espionage coups spring.

Using the Secret Services' resources for personal ends was out. It was frowned on even with people Upstairs, lamented with those who made visits up there, and condemned outright with those who, like Apple, didn't even know where to find the staircase.

A car came curving backwards towards him, wanting the slot. He looked at his watch as he strode over the kerb. The problem would have to wait, he thought.

Not in the slightest way returned to feeling a traitor, he assured himself, Apple hurried off in search of a taxi.

With another search, inside, for comfort and self-esteem, Apple mused jovially that he would get Ethel back in no time at all. Possibly the joyriders would bring her home themselves. If she had suffered a little dent here, a bit of a scratch there, he would take her back to the coachbuilder for cosmetic surgery.

Which—Ethel's paint job—brought to Apple for the first time a disturbing realisation. He wouldn't have been able to use Ethel on this mission anyway. Not on any mission. In appearance she was as discreet as ten drunken sailors in a cathedral.

It saddened Apple that he and Ethel would never work together on a caper. But, he thought, why couldn't he have her sprayed black again? A rapid, one-coat deal with non-permanent paint that could be washed off afterwards? He could. He should. He would. As soon as he got her safely back.

Cheered, Apple hurried on.

Earl's Court Exhibition Hall. Half a million square feet of floor space. Home of the International Motor Show and the Royal Tournament, among others. Opened in 1937. Properly called not "Hall" but "Building."

Reciting these intriguing facts to himself, Apple paid and passed through a turnstile. There was no need to scan around to see if Kate had arrived yet. She stood up in the crowd. He joined her.

As they exchanged muted greetings, Apple noticed that they were drawing considerable attention. He began to edge away, invitingly. Kate, like an expert dancer, obliged by following.

Soon they were on the sidelines, beside the first of the models. It was a rowboat standing on its nose to show off a mechanical rower. The height was a comfort.

Even so, Apple sagged at the knees while taking turns with Kate at watching the turnstiles. It felt weird, standing beside a woman who was nearly as tall as himself; weird because he didn't know if he was enjoying it or not.

Kate asked, "Are we going to fore-and-aft this scene, Basil, or twin along behind?"

To Apple it seemed obvious she was telling him that the first, being preferable under these circumstances, was the one they should follow. Smittenly, he mused that not only was Kate a pro, she had the kindness to offer her knowledge to him in the form of a question, as though they were equals, not old hand and tyro.

Apple helped her and thanked her by playing along, saying after a judicious grunt, "The old f-and-a, I think. It can't hurt to split up the double image."

"That's my opinion, Basil."

"When I did my training at Damian House—but maybe you went there as well?"

Kate gave her quiet smile. "Yes, I did. And I refreshed there not long ago." She went on to talk with fondness of the country mansion.

Apple, straightening, watched her face avidly. He was almost sure now that if she smiled fully there would be dimples. When she broke off her talk he was sorry, even though she next said, quietly, "Enter mark."

Apple looked around. Coming through a turnstile was the face from the photograph. It was on top of an untidy serge suit, drab shirt, limp twist of a tie. Alexander Grishin looked as dangerous as corn flakes.

"Pardon my dust," Kate murmured, moving off with a graceful swoop.

Apple sagged again and watched the Russian come forwards through the crowd. Grishin neared, passed and went on along one of the aisles between display stands.

Apple followed at a sensible distance. Far ahead he could see the mane of fair hair that was quickly becoming familiar. Kate cast glances aside and behind with excellent naturalness.

Alexander Grishin moved at the same pace as others in the sluggish stream of browsers. He paused to look at an automatic baby-changer, a gadget for straightening old nails and three rivals in the problem of getting the remains of preserves from behind the neck curve of their jars.

The procession went on. Nothing seemed to take the Russian's attention except the exhibits, at which he frequently stopped. Sole action was when he turned off onto another aisle. Apple waited at the junction until

Kate saw what happened. She started back and he went on, passing Grishin and becoming fore so that Kate was aft.

Half an hour later, after another direction change, they were once more in their original positions.

Alexander Grishin paused yet again. The exhibit that had taken his interest was a noisy working model whose purpose Apple could only guess at. It looked like a sewing machine with arms—skinny members that were scooping at air.

Other people were standing at the same place. On one side of Grishin, who lingered, was a woman. On his other side was a man. Young and fashionably dressed to the point of foppishness, the man stared at the model while chewing gum.

Apple knew about the gum routine. The chewing motion made fine camouflage for covert speech, especially if the speaker had a background of noise, like that being afforded by the working model.

Apple ambled closer. He stopped ten feet away, by a concrete pillar. Concentrating on the chewer's jaw rhythm, he decided that it could be out of sync. Alexander Grishin, however, had his mouth firmly closed and appeared to be intent on the machine.

Something made Apple look away, to the rear of where the Russian was standing. He was startled to see that he, the watcher, was being watched; and openly.

The man had the physique of a wrestler: no neck, vast shoulders and chest, crew-cut hair, broad flat face. His suit managed to be neat despite the strain on its seams.

If he's not a Hammer, Apple thought despondently, I'm not a linguist. He drooped against the pillar.

The big man was still watching. He made no effort to hide his interest. The only time he broke his gaze, and that briefly, was to look directly at Alexander Grishin.

Kate was waiting in the distance, Apple noted. Shortening his view, he saw the man he had code-named "Fashion-plate" turn casually aside and, still chewing, move on. Within seconds, Grishin followed.

Apple made to do the same. He held back as the big man took two steps towards him. A confrontation seemed to be in the offing.

When in doubt, do the unexpected—thus ran one of the adages they drummed into you at Damian House.

So Apple made a swift decision. He would play spy. He would play it so badly that they would know he couldn't possibly be one; that they would dismiss him as a fool or a man who was up to some peculiar game of his own.

Apple wasn't thinking of the mission's success so much as the fact that, if he were tumbled by the opposition, he would be pulled out like money from a fire. He had to stay in, if only because of Kate.

The big man came another step forwards.

Apple shot his eyes quickly all around. He brought out cigarettes as if the packet were a pistol. With his back rigidly to the pillar, he got out a cigarette and tossed the packet disdainfully away.

The big man was staring. Alexander Grishin was far on, still close behind Fashion-plate.

Raising the cigarette slowly, Apple scraped his back around the pillar. He gave a tough grimace, narrowed one eye, and almost put the cigarette in his right nostril.

The big man frowned.

Fumbling, Apple got the cigarette in his lips. He was too tense to be embarrassed. His tension grew and he stopped reaching for his lighter and he nearly groaned when the big man came striding across the aisle.

After shoving a browser out of his way, the man halted directly in front of Apple and clamped a weighty hand on his shoulder. The cigarette fell from Apple's lips.

Frown heavier, the big man said in grinding Cockney, " 'Ere, mate, didn't you used to work in Billingsgate?"

Apple flopped loose. His feelings turned to cold annoyance, at himself for having guessed wrong. He said, "No."

"That's right," the man said. "You and Fred and them."

"You're mistaken."

"And I've got the name now. It's Sid."

Apple tried to move away. The hand was more like concrete than the pillar. "You are in error, sir."

Grinning, the man said, "So it's you, Sid, eh? I fought it was."

Apple shook his head. "No."

"What you up to these days, Sid mate?"

"No."

"Doing real well meself. Still in the security lark. I'm working right this minute, tell you the trufe."

"Excuse me."

The hand stayed firm. "I been keeping a eye on a fella just over there. Gone now. Fella with a face like a ape."

"Oh?" Apple said.

"I 'appen to know who 'e is, if 'e only knew it—knew that I know, I mean. You know."

"Who is he?"

"One of the cleverest little shoplifters you'd ever wish to meet," the big man said. "Used to operate in Chelsea about ten years ago."

"I must be running along now."

"I got this gift, see, for remembering faces."

"Excuse me," Apple said. He sank abruptly from the hand and ducked under the arm. "Be good."

The crowd, denser here, was moving slowly. To make matters worse for Apple, every stand had its collection of browers, causing obstructions in the aisles. This area of the exhibition was devoted to gadgets that aided the home-brewer.

Alexander Grishin was nowhere to be seen.

Apple tried the impossible: hurrying without seeming to hurry. This he did by walking in sagged strides while holding his hands together and forwards like a plough. His smiling face stated that it had no connexion with the pushing below.

He saw Fashion-plate.

His jaw still chomping rhythmically, the overdressed man stood looking at an electric beer pump. It sounded like a Jeep stuck in mud.

Grishin absent, Apple wondered if he had guessed wrong there as well. The fop could merely be a noise freak. But the unmatched pair could also have had their meeting and now be easing away from the scene.

Just in case, Apple took in more details of Fashion-plate as he ploughed on by.

The next known person he saw was Kate. Leaning out from around an exhibit, she was beckoning to him. Only the fact of them both being tall, Apple reflected with satisfaction, even smugness, made visual contact possible above the crowd.

Kate's beckon became more urgent after she had glanced fleetingly behind her. Apple forged on. He gave up both on smile and sag and pushed like a tourist in a shrine.

When he reached Kate she said, "Alex just tried to leave by an emergency door. It was locked. I think he's gone on to find another."

"He's in a hurry?"

"Could be, but it doesn't look that way. Maybe he just wants to leave without having to go all the way to the front. Come on."

Apple followed along a side aisle. He told about Fashion-plate and the chewing. "Like this exit bit, it could be something and it might be nothing."

"Anyway," Kate said, "we're not without hope. Oops."

About to round a corner, she stopped abruptly. Apple, immediately behind, walked into her back. Briefly their bodies were pressed together and Apple's face was buried in the long fair hair.

Turning as she stepped clear, Kate said, "Sorry."

"It smells like a flower shop."

"What does?" She looked at the nearby stands.

"Tell you later," Apple mumbled quickly. "Why'd you stop?"

"He's there, at a door," Kate said. She peered around the corner. "Now you see him, now you don't."

"He's gone?"

"Yes. Let's go."

They hurried on towards the bleak wall which held a row of doors operated by push bars. Apple scanned around carefully in case the mark hadn't left, his action having been a trick.

Kate stopped by a door which, after a short pause, she began to open. When there was space enough, she looked out. "Yes," she said, pushing the door wider.

They went outside into darkness. Away to one side, as dramatic as a photographer's prize-winning entry, a figure walked in silhouette against a background of street brightness. Apple was unaware of his happy sigh.

He and Kate started to follow, keeping close to the wall. In whispers they agreed not to fore-and-aft this one. But might it not be better to stay apart, Apple suggested.

"How about if we're a courting couple?" Kate said, linking her arm through his. "If such an animal isn't extinct."

"Perfect," Apple said. "And I'm sure it isn't. You see them around from time to time."

"We'll send a donation to their protection society."

His sigh this time Apple was aware of. He thought he could go on walking like this for ever. It would do, however, if Alexander Grishin were decent enough to go on foot back to Oranger Lane, which appeared likely.

Five minutes later, on busy Warwick Road, the positioning of mark and twin tailers was unchanged. But Apple had several times had a familiar sensation across his shoulders.

He asked, "Do you get the body-word that you're being shadowed?"

"No, Basil, I don't. Not in the least."

"Then it's only paranoia," he joked, and didn't look back until they were at the next corner. He thought he saw, though wasn't sure, a man dodge out of sight; a dark man with a full beard.

The next corner after that, Alexander Grishin, who had shown no interest in the street behind him, went into a large pub. Apple and Kate halted at a distance.

"One of us ought to go in," Kate said. "Right?"

"You go. I'll I-spy in case of clever stuff."

She asked his favourite drink. He told her. She promised to have that one. "If our Alex stays in there long enough."

An hour and a half passed. For Apple, stimulated by Kate and the operation, it passed slowly. Yet he wasn't bored. Despite nothing happening, and no recurrence of the trailing finger, he managed to get enjoyment out of pacing and posing, trying out every doorway, looking innocent when people walked by and telling himself: *You're here. On a mission. This is it. Enjoy. You are definitely not bored.*

Finally, Alexander Grishin emerged from the pub and walked briskly away. When he was thirty yards distant, Kate came out. Apple joined her. Linking arms they began to walk.

Kate related a normal-sounding pub session. The Russian had drunk three pints of beer (to Kate's two sherries à la Apple), spoken passingly with the landlord, with an old man and with a youth who was looking for someone to play darts with; had bought a newspaper, eaten a meat pie, watched the news on television, looked at other people.

Kate concluded, "The poor man seemed lonely."

Apple, warmed, squeezed her arm. He was about to speak when he saw a complete change in the scene ahead. Alexander Grishin had turned. He was hurrying back.

Apple and Kate stopped. They swung face to face. They looked at one another. They blinked. They shrugged. They raised questioning eyebrows. They nodded.

With a smooth accord of movement, they slid into an embrace. Apple put his arms around Kate's waist, Kate put her arms around Apple's neck. They kissed.

Dimly, Apple was aware of footsteps approaching at a fast clip. Mediumly, he was alert to a trailing-finger sensation across his shoulders. Strongly, he was cognizant of the way Kate's body felt pressed against his own. Stridently, he was conscious of the soft warm lips that tasted of sherry.

The kiss went on, seemly yet sensuous. It, and to lesser degree the embrace, gradually gained prominence in Apple's awareness. The tactile was all. When it ended, when Kate eased back, Apple was slow to understand what was going on.

From a combination of Kate's whispers and the sight of Grishin swinging a white object as he once again walked ahead in his original direction, Apple gathered that the Russian had gone back to the pub to get the newspaper he had forgotten. He had taken no notice of the necking couple.

"Yes," Apple said vaguely.

He stayed in his smitten mistiness over the next ten minutes, until he was walking homeward alone. They had seen Alexander Grishin back to the overflow house, Apple knew, and had separated after agreeing to meet there in the morning at nine.

Sighing himself alert, Apple began to walk at a pace to suit his stimulation. Grinning like a pirate in the wind, he relived that embrace and those lips like two sherries.

As Apple opened the door of his flat, he saw an envelope lying on the threshold. He scooped it up indifferently and tossed it onto the hatstand shelf.

The note, he expected, would be from Mrs. 3B, inviting him to one of her cultural teas. Or from Miss 2C, saying she was glad to hear that he had got over his yelping cough (Monico). Or it would be a letter of complaint from the landlord, who felt slighted that Apple never had anything to grumble about.

At his writing desk in the living room, Apple set up his typewriter. He rolled in paper. Forcing himself with effort to think spy, not lover, he started to type out a report on the evening's activities.

He named each of the gadgets that Alexander Grishin had shown particular interest in. He told about the incident with Fashion-plate, whom he described in detail. He gave a second-hand description of Grishin's doings in the pub, not leaving out the newspaper and the meat pie, for anything that changed hands was always suspect.

Leaning back, Apple wondered about that newspaper. Would someone like Grishin, whose English was imperfect, bother to retrace his steps to get something that had cost so little? He would have to discuss it with Kate.

Kate. Apple got up and started to wander around the room, smittening away strongly.

Soon, told by a belch that he was hungry, Apple made for the kitchen, humming as he went. In the hall he performed a military turn and marched dutifully to the hatstand. He picked up and opened the envelope.

Apple's face widened in surprise. The piece of paper he was holding had an uneven scattering of words which were of different sizes and different style type. They had been cut out individually from newsprint.

Apple read the message over and over again. It took him a long time to digest the fact that Ethel had been abducted and was being held for ransom.

CHAPTER 2

When in his flat, Apple generally wore a tartan robe. It gave him peace, though it looked about as peaceful as Saturday night in a Dublin bar: the colours screamed, the checks were a foot square.

But the robe served Apple indoors the way Ethel did out. It answered his need to rebel against the conformity which his professional life demanded and his shyness encouraged. It told him he was strong, not timid. In a way, it took the form of a security blanket, tailored.

This morning, Apple had more need than ever of his robe. He held it close to him with self-hugging arms as he wandered around the flat.

He slouched, tired. Last night he had slept fitfully, having been disturbed by thoughts of Ethel. He was thinking about her still.

Apple was aware of the carnap racket. It was common, though less so than dognapping, which flourished in pet-loving Britain as nowhere else. For one thing, it wasn't so easy to bring off; a dog could be picked up in the arms or snagged under a net or shot with a tranquiliser dart, whereas a car had to be rendered driveable, with all the dangers of regular theft. For another thing, a smallish animal could be kept almost anywhere, while a vehicle needed large, secret accommodation.

The rackets were alike, however, Apple knew, in that the abducted entity didn't necessarily have to be pedigreed or expensive, just beloved, as bespoken by the obvious care taken of dog or car.

Owners usually cooperated. They paid the ransom without fuss, though car owners were more likely to go to the police. Pet owners, the danger over, contented themselves with membership in one of the societies that campaigned to have flogging brought back for dognappers, those same groups who advocated leniency for rapists and kindness for muggers.

Apple stopped thinking of English eccentricity. He told himself in irritation to get off the general and back to the particular. What, in fine, was he going to do?

That was simple enough: nothing. There was nothing he could do, except hope that Ethel was being looked after and would be returned safely once he had paid the blood money.

Apple was relieved that the moral question of whether to pay up, thus compounding a felony, or go to the police, as a good citizen should, had been taken out of his hands. The mission ruled out any contact with the authorities.

The precise amount of money to be extracted would be discussed when contact was made, the note said. Apple would be telephoned—no time stated. His number, obviously, they had obtained from his car papers.

Apple looked at his watch. In thirty minutes or so he would have to leave to meet Kate. What if the carnappers didn't call before then? What if, getting no answer later, they decided to hell with it and either sold Ethel to a junkyard or abandoned her to her fate? Just how professional were these people? Were they sincere?

For the dozenth time Apple brought out the letter and searched the wording for nuance or clues. As always before, he learned nothing, but did conclude that the care taken in fashioning the letter ruled out an amateur or a crank.

He roamed, sighed, fretted. He wished Monico were here so they could talk the problem over. Whenever he slouched into the living room he stared accusingly at the telephone.

Apple went dispiritedly to dress. He put on the suit he had worn yesterday to work. Which reminded him that he had yet to ask for leave of absence for the duration of the mission.

Minutes later Apple was dialling the United Kingdom Philological Institute. Keep it short, he warned himself. The corrupt bastards might try and call while you're talking.

Connected with his superior, niceties over, Apple said, "I know this is short notice, sir, but I'd like to take some time off. I feel the sudden need of a holiday. Somewhere abroad."

"Why, of course, my boy," Professor Warden said. "I understand perfectly. You're going to do a bit of—um—"

"Hunting, sir?"

"No no. Nothing like that. You can't fool me. You're planning to do a little—er—ah—"

"Fishing, professor?"

"No, my boy. *Spying.* That's the word."

Apple stared into space, the other worry forgotten. He said hollowly, "I beg your pardon, sir?"

"Yes yes, Porter, I see it all. You can't pull the wool over my eyes. I wasn't born yesterday, y'know."

"I'm afraid I don't understand, sir."

"I know you, you see, my boy. You're not one to let the grass grow under your feet. Obviously, you want to go to Switzerland. You want to have a personal look into the Romansh situation."

Apple blew out noisily with relief. Cutting into Professor Warden's enthusiasm, he covered without actually giving a negative or an affirmative, although he did offer philological hope by hinting that languages flourished better under threat than with encouragement. He disconnected.

Apple stood beside the table, glaring down at the telephone. Ring, you idiot, he willed. The instrument stayed dumb. Bloody lunatic, Apple thought, walking away gruffly.

The telephone rang.

Apple doubled back like whiplash. At the last second, before grabbing up the receiver, he froze. He had foreknowledge of farce. He could see himself knocking the instrument over in his haste, fighting clownishly to claim the handset, gabbling into it like a frantic child.

The call signal was still giving its regular bursts. Apple drew in a long, long breath. He let it out while reaching to the receiver and raising it to his face. In a dull voice he quoted his number.

A female voice asked, "Am I addressing Mr. Appleton Porter?"

"You are."

"I am calling in connexion with the letter you ought to have received by now."

The voice, Apple noted, was as depersonalised as the note. Apart from the certainty that the caller was female, there were no clues, no way of judging age or accent. Words were pronounced robot style.

Apple took heart at the caution, the professionalism, the suggestion that these people would do nothing rash or spiteful. He decided to try a bluff.

"Which letter?" he said. "I get dozens of 'em. Who is this, please?"

The woman said, "The letter about your car."

Laughing: "Oh, that one. About my old banger. Yes, I enjoyed reading it."

"The car is not of value to you?"

"Not a fat lot."

"In that case," the caller said, "we will break it up for the spare parts and the non-ferrous metal."

Apple gasped, "Wait. Hold on. Stop a minute." He gave up on bluff.

"I do not have all day to wait. Nor do I intend to be kept talking while this call is traced."

"No one's tracing the call."

"Good. You would be foolish to bring the police into this."

"No police," Apple said, beaten. "How much?"

With a hint of importance, the woman said, "One thousand pounds."

Apple gaped. "You can't be serious. A thousand? That's ridiculous. Absurd. And anyway I haven't got a thousand quid." That was true; he only had nine hundred and seventy in his account.

"How much have you got?"

Shrewdly: "Five hundred."

The woman countered, "Borrow another four hundred and you will get your car back."

"I might be able to borrow one hundred. No more. So six is the best I can do."

"Tell you what. Listen. I will make you a deal. We will let this article go for eight hundred. Not a penny less. That is my final word."

"Can't do it," Apple said, proud of his courage. "Six is as high as I can go."

In a menacing tone the woman said, "Spare parts."

"No more than six hundred."

"Non-ferrous metal."

"Six hundred and fifty," Apple said. "And that's the end."

Surprisingly and gratifyingly the woman said, "A deal."

"Good. When and where?"

"We will let you know that later. Meanwhile prepare the cash. Old notes only. Good-bye. You will be contacted."

It was a good omen, Apple mused, that despite every-thing he was first on the scene—though only just. As he turned back from having walked along Oranger Lane, he saw Kate in a car. She was reversing it into a parking space at the kerb.

Apple headed for the black Ford Fiesta. He was emo-tionally on a seesaw in respect of the carnapping. All signs pointed to him getting Ethel back and the money was unimportant, but he didn't like the situation and kept returning to the search for a way of outwitting the carnappers. He had a dark suspicion, which he declined to recognise fully, that even with the ransom paid he might never see Ethel again.

Apple reached the driver's door as Kate switched off the motor. He said, "Good morning."

"Morning, Basil," Kate said with her distant smile. "It looks as if it's going to pour down any minute."

Apple absently upped his palms. "So it does."

"Get in. We might as well watch from here, don't you think?"

"Of course." He went around to the other side. Squeezing down and inside, he noticed the gabardine dress last, after a decent pair of knees and the start of promising thighs.

Kate said, "It looks less mysterious in daylight."

The overflow house stood across the street and farther along. Like all its neighbours in the unbroken row, it was flat-faced and without frontage. The trim's green be-longed in an institution. Flower boxes stuck out from the fourth-floor windows like too many eyebrows.

Apple nodded. "As dull as our Alex."

"Who's due out any time now. If he's playing it straight today, he'll go to the Red Shed and stay at least until noon, when he might or might not go out for lunch. Same routine until six o'clock."

Apple, who had never heard the Soviet Embassy called that before, repeated it to himself with delight before asking about last night's newspaper transaction.

"An old woman," Kate said. "As straight as a die."

"How could you tell?"

"The way she sidled up to Grishin. You would've thought she was slipping him blueprints of a secret weapon. No agent would be so stagey and obvious."

Apple cleared his throat. He said it didn't look as if it was going to rain after all.

Weather was still the subject of their conversation when Alexander Grishin appeared, the latest of several people to come out of the overflow house. He wore a raincoat, which, after a careful look at the sky, he took off and folded over his arm.

Kate said, "He's crossing to this side."

"But then he'll go the other way, surely, for the bus or the underground."

"He could be in a walking mood. He was last night."

And was again this morning, evidently, for he turned towards the car on reaching the pavement.

Apple and Kate tensed, as though waiting for a collision. Staring ahead at the approaching Russian, they went through a rapid exchange.

Kate: "We shouldn't let him see us."

Apple, nodding: "He might've registered us last night, vaguely, and make a connexion if he spots us again this close."

Kate: "So we split up?"

Apple: "It's too late. He'd see the action. See the memorable tallness if not the face, whichever one of us got out."

Kate: "What else is there?"

Apple: "We could neck."

Kate: "That's a repeat. A reminder."

Apple: "What if we bend down, pretend to be looking at something on the floor?"

Kate: "Wouldn't that look suspicious?"

Apple: "You're right, it would."

Kate: "What we need is a diversion."

Apple: "My mind's a blank."

Alexander Grishin was mere yards away. Abruptly, Kate whipped around, reaching a hand towards the back seat. What she pulled forwards onto her lap was a travelling rug. After roughing it quickly into an elongated bundle; she fumbled at the neck of her dress.

Although Apple began to understand, he still felt surprise that it was going to happen. Fascinated, he watched as Kate swiftly opened her dress almost to the waist, reached inside and eased one of her breasts out into full, piquant view.

Her head lowered, the bundled blanket cradled high, Kate appeared to be letting a baby have a rest between bouts of nursing.

After a fast, sidelong glance at the nearly-here Russian, Apple also lowered his head, face towards the maternity scene, which, he assured himself, he had to do to make the picture look natural.

Apple stared wistfully, cheerfully, erotically and judiciously at the smooth white breast with its centre point of pink thrust. He gave it a 9.

Apple was having a fine time. An additional boost was the fact that the blush which had threatened, cowed by his pleasure, had stayed below the level of his collar.

"Phew," Kate said. Straightening, she thrust her breast back inside with a firmness that made Apple twitch. He looked around. Alexander Grishin had passed and was walking on.

"He had a good gander," Kate said. She tossed the blanket over her shoulder. "I think we did it."

"You did it, you mean. Brilliant."

"Too bad I can't take the credit, Basil. I learned the routine at Damian House."

"I don't remember that one."

Buttoning her dress, Kate smiled, this time with more warmth than usual. The suggestion of dimples was stronger. She said, "I doubt if they bother to teach it to the male students."

Apple laughed. He asked, "But what made you remember it?"

"In the pub last night. I saw how our Alex looked at the women."

The Russian, Apple thought, couldn't be all bad. He said, brisk, asserting himself in his role, "I'll aft, and you fore in the car, okay?"

"Check."

The tailing was an anticlimax. Nothing happened. It didn't even rain. Alexander Grishin walked to Kensington Palace Gardens and disappeared inside the Soviet Embassy. Going on, Apple joined Kate in her black Fiesta.

"Well," he said, "that's that until midday. What do we do now?"

"Let's think about it as we drive."

They went along Bayswater Road and discussed useful ways of killing time. Kate handled the car in that seemingly careless way of a first-class driver. Apple's smittenship thrived.

Soon, Kate turned off Park Lane into Mayfair. She mentioned that she could always go and get a manicure.

Apple said, "I have an idea. If, that is, the countryside appeals to you."

Kate turned to him quickly. "Oh, it does. I love the open country. I don't see enough of it."

He told himself he might have known, told Kate about his cottage. "I have something to attend to down there, so it might as well be now. We have double the necessary time to get there and back, with no rush in between."

"Talk about brilliant ideas. Please point me in the right direction."

Apple yelled, "Stop!"

The whole process, from first glimpse to raucous yell, had taken mere seconds.

Apple had seen the pale-blue hair, next the face with its foxy eyes, and had placed the woman immediately despite her being dressed now in a trouser suit. He had added that the voice on the telephone was female. He had seen it anew as odd, improbable, the way she had stopped him yesterday afternoon when he was leaving the Institute. That, the delaying tactic, coupled with the image change from Mrs. Suburbia to Ms. Mayfair, had been the prime mover.

Kate, looking scared, had screeched the Fiesta to a halt, causing another screech of brakes behind. Apple flung open the door. He got out with a snapped:

"I'll explain later. Got to go. Sorry I startled you. Go back to base. I'll call you soonest. Okay?" Not waiting for an answer he slammed the door and hurried to the pavement.

Being tall, Apple had no trouble seeing well ahead over the dense trundle of pedestrians. The woman with blue-rinse hair was as before, moving in the other direction, strolling along close to the kerb.

Apple kept the same distance back. Settling from his urgency, as well as from the jolt of what he had so rapidly deduced/assumed, he thought again about that delaying ploy in front of the Institute.

Ethel's ignition wiring being sealed; the only way she could be started illicitly was by somebody trying one by one the car thief's ninety-nine keys, which were carried on a wire loop. This took time. So, while the trying went on, an accomplice went to the owner's place of work to run interference.

How did they know where he worked?—from the car papers. How did they know what he looked like?—by asking someone inside if Mr. Porter was that bald man who . . .

It was a bit thin, Apple admitted. But plumper when you realised that the idea wasn't to lift Ethel at once, which hadn't happened, but only to find the right key. Then the theft could be pulled off at a convenient time, in a day or a week or a month.

Although it still wasn't fleshy, Apple had an instinctive feeling that he was on the right track. In any case, he had nothing to lose by the shadowing.

Ms. Mayfair strolled on. She had both hands in the coat pockets of her trouser suit, which, Apple could tell by the cut, was by no means a cheap item.

It occurred to him that the woman could even be a brilliant pickpocket, the thief's ninety-nine keys not having been involved. While talking to him, she had dipped his car key, taken a wax impression and put it back again.

Apple smiled grimly. The idea was no longer skinny.

After turning a corner, the woman moved in beside the elegant stores. She looked in their windows as she walked, but randomly. The impression she gave was that she had seen it all before.

She went into a beauty salon. Apple accepted with resignation that he was in for a long wait. However, before he could select a good, unobtrusive pitch, Ms. Mayfair came out again. She turned his way.

In two long strides Apple was off the kerb and in the narrow space between parked cars. Bending horizontal from the hips he peered at the bumper.

He counted off thirty seconds, the while not attempting to glance up. Which made him wonder if he was playing this right. He was performing like a spy, when maybe he ought to be acting your average citizen. Should he grab the woman and accuse her of being the carnapper?

No, Apple decided quickly. He told himself that was the wrong tactic altogether—while ignoring the knowledge that his decision was based partly on his horror of creating a public scene.

A voice grated, "May I help you?"

Semi-straightening, seeing a well-dressed man with folded arms and a tight mouth, Apple said, "No, I was wrong. It isn't a Colorado beetle." He reversed out of the space.

Ms. Mayfair was nicely ahead. Following, Apple stayed in the roadway between parked and moving cars. He presumed that the call at the beauty shop had been a failed try at getting service, which meant that she would be going to other establishments of the same type.

Again Apple was wrong. The woman hailed a cab. She got in without a backwards glance and the cab moved off.

Apple looked around for another taxi. Although there were plenty, none had their hire signs lit up. But the traffic was moving at the downtown dribble and halt, so Apple knew he was in no immediate danger of losing his mark.

Repeating ten times the licence number of Ms. Mayfair's cab, Apple followed it at a steady walk along two streets. He began to envision being led to a sinister building where he would find Ethel, her back bumper chained to the wall.

The taxi turned onto Piccadilly, went from sight. When Apple, not hurrying, reached the corner, he saw that the roadway had few vehicles. The cab was well ahead. He began to run.

Traffic lights helped. Apple was able to reduce the gap before green let the taxi go on again. This shrink-and-stretch routine continued, with Apple staying in the roadway and with vehicles all around him. He ignored stares and beeps.

Ms. Mayfair's taxi swept around Piccadilly Circus, alone, having gone through a red and left other cars behind. Apple was also alone as he loped around the island. He drew a lot of attention. Much of it was patently amused. He told himself he didn't care and that for two pins he would go around the island again.

On the straight, Apple speeded up. It was necessary, he thought, and had nothing to do with the way the increased breeze felt on his burning face.

The tailing went on. With more stretch than shrink, Apple chased along Pall Mall, around Trafalgar Square and down the Strand. He cursed buses that got in his way and tutted at examples of bad driving.

By the time Ms. Mayfair's cab started on Fleet Street, Apple was suffering. His heart thudded, his lungs heaved, his legs felt like dead eels.

A car drew level. Leaning out, its driver asked, "Taxi, guv'nor?" Apple ignored what he took to be a gibe. But, as the car moved on, he realised that it was a minicab, a pirate in the trade. He gathered enough breath to shout, "Wait!"

Within seconds he was heaped on the back seat and the small car was moving off. Looking aside, the driver asked, "Destination, guv?" He had long hair and an earring.

"Follow that cab."

"Everyone says that. Everyone's real funny. I laugh meself sick all day long."

"I mean it," Apple said. "My wife's in there with my best friend."

The driver said, "Couldn't be worse." He increased speed. "But I know a couple of rentable telephone numbers if you're so inclined."

"No, thanks. Just keep the taxi in sight without getting too close."

"Leave it to me, guv."

Over the following ten minutes, Apple politely declined information on Japanese pornography, Lebanese marijuana, Portuguese masseuses and a Cockney who would beat the crap out of anyone for fifty quid.

Somewhere in Spitalfields, Ms. Mayfair's taxi went from sight around a bend. When the minicab, following with caution in this traffic-sparse area, was taking the bend also, Apple saw the taxi coming back. He checked the number again to be sure. Ms. Mayfair wasn't inside.

"Stop here," Apple said urgently. He looked all around with fast darts of his head. There was nothing to be seen of the woman with blue hair.

The district was a new residential-shopping complex. From each corner of the shop-lined mall rose a high-rise of flats. There were dozens of businesses, hundreds of homes.

Although knowing that Ms. Mayfair could be in her taxi, crouched down, Apple saw that as by far the smallest of the two possibilities. Here, or close nearby, was where the woman would be found.

As Apple reached for the car door handle, six mountaineers began to tap-dance on the cab roof. The rain, which had been increasing its threat steadily, had started with a smug and violent flourish.

Apple decided to leave the search for now. He didn't want to be rushed by adverse weather. Relaxing, he asked the driver to take him back.

"I told you it wouldn't last long."

"Too bad. I like rain in the country."

"So do I. It makes everything smell so fab."

"And in town it just makes everything smell."

Kate, driving her Fiesta, switched off the windscreen

wipers. Apple was glad. The steady *woosh-click* might have sent him to sleep if it had gone on much longer. Turning to look out at the fields, he smothered a yawn.

Apple had telephoned Kate from a box at Marble Arch. She had joined him in fifteen minutes, her greeting an eager, "What was that all about?"

The story Apple had created in the minicab and while waiting. With his ankles crossed he had said, "A caper I was on some time ago. I can't go into details, as you know. But I can tell you that the Reds were operating a combined massage parlour and porno shop, with international staff, as a contact station, which came to light when a dope peddler got beaten up and robbed of fifty pounds."

"Sounds fascinating."

"One of the non-Russian people got away, and that's whom I thought I saw in Mayfair. I was mistaken." He had given himself 10 for invention in the minicab, had reduced it to 8 at Marble Arch, had come down to 6 after giving his story.

The car zipped along country roads. Apple and Kate talked safely; that is, on subjects which gave away nothing of their backgrounds. They went from the new movies to the latest political mess, from the shocking price of things to the difficulties of being tall. Apple liked Kate's honesty. He thought at one stage, sighing mentally: all right, 5.

The cottage, an inheritance, was semi-pseudo-ancient. It had been built out of old material in the thirties. Low and bulgy, it had a bow window and the kind of weeds that could pass for flowers.

Apple took Kate inside. She enthused about the beams, chintz, brassware and rocking chairs. After putting a match to the ready-laid fire, Apple left her and set off to accomplish the trip's dual purpose: to see Monico and introduce him to Kate.

The farm lay two fields away. Midway across the second, Apple gave a piercing hiss. The next moment a tall, thin, ginger-coloured dog burst through the hedge and came bounding forwards.

Monico was a Podenco Ibizenco, a breed peculiar to the Balearic island of Ibiza. He looked like a greyhound that had not been very well lately.

As ungainly in manner as he was timid in nature, Monico fell over twice during the exuberant meeting, though he got up without any help. His tail wagged vertically as well as from side to side. He yelped often but produced no barks.

A face looked over the hedge. It was florid to the point of being unnerving. Eyebrows met in the middle over a bulbous nose, which topped a broad mouth. Above all was a green mangle that looked something like a hat.

Farmer Galling said, accusingly, "I thought you was at death's door."

"One of the new miracle drugs, Mr. Galling," Apple said. "I'm fit enough to be out of bed for a few hours."

"Me, I've always fancied having a good long illness. Be nice to get away from it all."

Hastily, before Galling could get started on one of his tirades against climate, government, insects and neighbours, Apple asked how Monico was getting along.

"Fair," the farmer said with red reluctance. "Be better when he gets used to the stock."

"I hope he's not being a nuisance."

"A bit. He's giving the hens and sheep ideas above their station."

"Really?"

"See, they chase him all over the place."

Apple said, "Well, I'm sorry about that, Mr. Galling."

The head lolled a shrug. "He'll be all right, that there animal of yours, once he settles down and stops not barking."

Apple got away. He retraced his steps with Monico frisking around him like a freaky pup. At the back of the cottage Apple stopped. Squatting, he got his dog to sit beside him. In a low voice he told about the crisis with Ethel.

It was a relief, having someone to talk to about his problem. He would have liked to have told Kate, but felt that, being such a hardened pro, she might consider his affection for a car to be foolish, which would set him back in the romance stakes.

Solemn now, Monico followed Apple inside, where he acted interested while the introduction was made. Though he swayed, he kept his balance when Kate shook his paw.

Apple made coffee. He and Kate sat in rocking chairs to drink it. Monico, sprawled in front of the fire, gnawed politely at a week-old bone.

At a glimpsed movement on the lane outside, Apple looked through the bow window. He saw, fleetingly, a man. The sole catchable detail was that the man had a beard.

Hardly aware of speaking aloud, Apple said, "Disguise?"

Kate lowered her coffee mug. "Yes, Basil, I've been going to suggest that. It might help us if we keep changing our appearances during this caper. Good for you."

Apple smiled, shy but proud. He told himself he was keeping up his end very well. He said, "We can start now, be ready for the one o'clock stint at the Red Shed. Shadow me."

They went to a mammoth wardrobe in one of the bedrooms. Coughing at the stench of mothballs, chuckling at the old-time styles, they sorted through Porter family clothing and tried on various garments.

Apple, reluctantly declining a top hat, settled for a shooting jacket and a green eyeshade. Kate chose a cloche hat plus a coat which had belonged to a great-aunt who had been five feet ten inches tall, a remarkable height for a woman sixty years ago.

After Apple had ashed down the fire, he took Monico back over the fields. He settled soberly from the fun of dressing up. Patting his dog with ersatz cheer, he explained that time flew and it would be weekend again in no time at all. He eased Monico through a hole in the hedge and strode away without looking back.

Wearing their disguises, Apple and Kate set off for the return drive to London. They decided to play the old spy game called "What to Do When," the winner in which was the one who came up with the most useless or inappropriate answer.

Apple began it with, "What do you say when someone sticks a gun in your back?"

"I gave at the office."

Apple said, "A little to the right, please, and scratch really hard."

"Harry? Joe? Fred?"

"If you wake the children . . ."

The game went on. Kate kept declaring Apple the winner, while he insisted that she was being generous. Apple was smitten, smitten.

At five minutes to one they were parked, illegally, on Bayswater Road within sight of where their mark would emerge. He hadn't done so by a quarter past.

Apple asked, "What do you say when somebody offers to take you to lunch?"

"Thank you very much."

Coat and eyeshade off, he went into his Bloomsbury bank just before it closed. The clerk seemed to find nothing peculiar in his request for old notes, which was a relief to Apple, who had vaguely expected to meet with suspicion, perhaps even be sent in to see the manager. He had prepared three stories for such an eventuality.

With the six hundred and fifty pounds distributed in various pockets, Apple headed briskly for Harlequin Mansions. A siesta was his intention, the wine at lunch having doubled his tiredness.

It had been a fun meal, at one of those small places in Soho where the French accents were as real as the French cooking. The odd clothing had helped.

They had talked shop briefly, agreeing that, as constant image change could do no harm, they would ring the changes again for the I-spy that began at six o'clock. They would wear tracksuits. That they already owned the necessary garments, were both fans of jogging, Apple chalked up as another strong sign that he and Kate were meant for each other.

Apple did wish, however, that Kate would lose some of her reserve, that she could become more relaxed, more animated and let her smile have full play. Maybe when the caper was over . . .

In respect of the lunch, the only niggle for Apple was whether or not he should put the cost on his mission expense account. It had been during work hours, true, but it had been more pleasure than business.

Not, he decided, slamming the flat door behind him hard. Feeling annoyingly honest, he went straight to the bedroom, where he flopped down just as he was and sank immediately into sleep.

He was awakened by the telephone. About to ignore the ringing, return to the dream of Kate and moonlight, he sat bolt upright on remembering Ethel. He leapt off the bed and ran raggedly into the living room.

As previously, Apple calmed himself before picking up the receiver. He said, "Appleton Porter speaking."

A familiar voice asked, "Do you have the money ready?"

"I have."

"Excellent. Then listen carefully. The rendezvous is Primrose Hill, on the road beside the park. Do you know where it is?"

"I do," Apple said. He resisted adding that he also knew the new complex in Spitalfields.

The woman said, "You must be there, alone, on foot, at seven this evening."

Apple asked, "Can't we make it earlier, perhaps at five?"

"It is after five o'clock now."

"Oh."

"And darkness is preferred," the woman said. "Therefore the time is seven. Take it or leave it."

"I'll take it."

"The money you will place in a large envelope, which you will hold in your hand. You will wait on the park side of the road. A car will come along, moving slowly. It will dip its lights several times as it approaches. On it coming level with you, you will see that the rear window is rolled down. You will toss the envelope through the window. Is all that clear?"

"Yes, perfectly."

"Good afternoon." The line clicked to deadness.

Apple attacked his writing desk. No large envelopes. He went out and ran to the nearest stationers. It was closed, but the proprietor was still there and, Apple being a regular customer, opened up willingly and sold him what he wanted.

Back home, while preparing a neat, flat packet of money, Apple worked out his escape excuse. He would tell Kate that he had a headache, but would be fine so long as it didn't get worse, which sometimes happened. When rendezvous time was getting near, he would say that the pain had grown. He had to go—not because he couldn't stand the pain but because it rendered him less than one hundred percent efficient. That would be a nice pro touch.

Although Apple didn't like the idea of lying to Kate, he allowed it and forgave himself on account of it being in an extremely good cause.

Hastily, he showered. When dry he taped the envelope onto his chest. He put on his jogging outfit after telephoning for a taxi, which was waiting when he emerged into the street. Minutes later he paid off the driver at Lancaster Gate.

Apple smiled on seeing another jogger coming towards him, exchanged the smile for a frown when he drew closer to Kate.

They stopped. Apple, trying not to overact agony, told about his headache. Kate was solicitous. She insisted that she should do the watching and that Apple should wait in the car, which she had parked off the main road.

"After all, Basil, the thuds of jogging can only make your headache worse."

"Let's hope it goes away."

Apple, given the keys, went and sat in the Fiesta. Almost at once Kate appeared at the corner, waving. He started the car and drove off. On Bayswater Road, going slowly, he saw Kate's tall figure doing a jog that was more up and down than forwards. Alexander Grishin would be strolling somewhere ahead.

After stopping twice so that he would stay well behind, Apple finally steered into Oranger Lane. He found a place to park. It was too far back from the overflow house to be useful, but was the only spot vacant.

Kate came to the window. "You stay here, Basil. I'll track back and forth."

"No," Apple said. "I'll do my share. We'll take turns, starting now."

For half an hour they swapped sessions of sitting and running, the latter a jog along one side of the street and back up the other. Apple looked at his watch more often than he looked at the overflow house.

At twenty minutes to seven, coming dusk, he made his last run. By the car he said, "You were right. The jogging's made my head feel like it's going to explode."

"Poor Basil," Kate said, gazing up sympathetically. She patted his arm.

Although tempted to milk the situation for more of the same, maybe a cool hand on the brow, Apple was overruled by his urgency. He said he had better get home to bed.

Kate asked, "How about disguises for tomorrow? May I suggest something?"

"By all means."

"I know where I can borrow a wheelchair and a nurse's uniform. We could play nurse and invalid."

Apple, who would have agreed to playing Tarzan and Jane, said, "Of course, of course. See you somewhere here tomorrow just before eight."

"No, at noon. Tomorrow's Sunday. Our Alex works a six-day week. If he does go out on Sundays, it's at around midday, Mr. Watkin told me."

"Ah yes," Apple said. "I knew this headache would dull my mind."

"Off you go, Basil. Good night."

"Good night, Kate."

Walking away slowly, as suited a man with a splitting headache, Apple realised that he didn't have to wait until the next day to see Kate again. With the business over Ethel settled, say in an hour or less, he could come back here, report that his pain had gone.

Having turned the corner, Apple burst into full-out running. He kept a watch on the traffic for vacant taxis. He saw none. And the possibility decreased when now he felt splashes of water on his face. It was raining.

Apple ran hard, heading northeast. He didn't think

about time. What he did think, nearing Paddington, was that he could get an underground train to Regent's Park, thus halving the distance. But what if the trains were running slow?

He saw a cab. Stationary, it was unloading passengers. Apple waited about ditheringly until everyone had alighted. He slammed inside, snapped out his destination and flopped on the seat.

Wiping a hand over his sodden hair, Apple decided to keep the cab waiting at Primrose Hill. He might not get another, and there was no use risking catching a heavy cold or even pneumonia.

After asking the driver and getting his accord on that, Apple unzipped the top of his tracksuit. He brought out the envelope of money. It was damp on both sides—rain and sweat.

At three minutes to seven the cab turned the last corner. On one side of the road were buildings, on the other the park's railings.

Apple said, "Turn down a side street and stop, please."

The driver obeyed. Getting out, Apple went back onto the main road, which had no pedestrians and little traffic. Rain bounced off the tarmac, flashing silver in the street lighting.

It was a drab scene; yet Apple, despite his concern over Ethel, started to see it as worthy of the situation, the dramatic passing over of ransom money. He looked around with steely eyes while walking back and forth along a stretch of pavement beside the park rails.

The envelope he held slightly away from his body, in prominence. That he knew about, but was unaware of giving the packet a small jiggle every time a car approached on his side of the road. No car dipped its headlights.

Seven o'clock came and went. By five past the hour, Apple's eyes were more like cast iron than steel. They had lost all their hardness by a quarter past. His sense of drama gone, he stood leaning drearily against the rails. Both he and the envelope were sodden.

At seven-thirty Apple gave up. He squelched back to the taxi. As he got in, the rain stopped, which made him laugh harshly. He gave his home address.

Soon Apple was soaking in a hot bath. Physical discomfort gone, some of the heat started to penetrate his spirits. He told himself not to despond in respect of Ethel. She would be safe. Tonight's non-show of the carnappers could be for a dozen reasons, from a flat tyre to illness. The woman might even have tried to contact him by telephone to call the rendezvous off.

Apple, cold and wet, had changed his mind about returning to the overflow house. Now, out of the bath, Apple warm and dry changed his mind again. He began to dress.

Wearing jeans, a dark sweater and slip-on shoes which, as with all his footwear, had the absolute minimum of heel, Apple turned into Oranger Lane. At once he saw that the black Fiesta had gone. To be sure, he walked the length of the street. No Kate.

Alexander Grishin had come out and Kate had followed, Apple thought. He hoped she would be all right. He hoped the Russian would simply go to the movies. He hoped the movie would be something—well—decent. He hoped Kate wouldn't get sat next to some nuisance or pervert.

And what you really hope, Apple chided himself, is that nothing of interest happens, especially not the answer to what Grishin is up to. You want to be in on every development.

Apple hoped there was nothing wrong with that.

He told himself: *you think more of the mission than you do of Kate.*

Apple denied this and told himself: *you don't sound very convinced.*

The exchange went on. It ended when Apple realised that he was standing at the mouth of an alley, which he recognised as the one that ran behind the overflow house.

Well now, he thought.

The alley was dark. Faint, patchy illumination came from the occasional lighted window in the rear upper floors of the houses. On either side, small backyards were separated from the service lane by a wall. Seven feet tall, punctuated by gates, the walls ran the alley's full length.

Apple entered at an amble, his hands clasped behind. He mused that Kate could, of course, have simply given up waiting and gone home. Being a pro, she would know whether or not it was the right move to make. Alexander Grishin, therefore, could still be in the house.

Apple walked on. He peered at numbers on the solid, door-type gates. Humming quietly, he reflected that it couldn't hurt if he was to snoop about a bit. He might pick up a clue that could lead Kate and him to the answer.

The gate at which Apple stopped, one third of the way along the alley, belonged to the overflow house. The heavy slab of wood bore no number, but the numbers of neighbours gave the game away, as did the dark green paint.

There was no one about. The area was essentially silent, the only sounds coming faintly from outside: traffic, an airplane, distant children.

Apple tried the handle. It didn't move. Nor was there any give when he pushed on the wood. Without needing to stretch, he reached up to the wall's top. It was formed like a miniature roof, sloping to an apex.

Better if it had been flat, Apple thought, but reminded

himself that it could have been a lot worse—topped with barbed wire or broken glass.

Putting both hands over the apex he began to haul himself up, his toes helping. When his shoulders had risen level with his grip, he threw up a leg and got the foot over the top. Five seconds later he was sitting there.

In the yard below him Apple could see only vague, dark shapes. The ground floor of the house was in darkness, while those windows on the upper floors which did have light were heavily curtained.

Cautiously, his mind closed to the idea of booby traps, Apple started to let himself down into the yard. His face was to the wall. He slowed descent even more as he neared the ground.

Apple's down-pointed, groping toes touched cement. He eased down flat-footed, let go of the wall and turned with a smile of satisfaction.

He fell over. What tripped him was a garbage can. This he knew by the stink and the noise. He gasped at both, but seriously so at the second.

The racket clanged and boomed on, while Apple, on his hands and knees, scrambled after the rolling, spilling can to try and seize it into silence.

The house door opened—fast. Into the doorframe moved a male figure. Backed by the dim light inside, all that could be discerned of the man was his largeness.

With a flung embrace, Apple claimed the garbage can. He set it upright on its own spillage. His shoes mashed onto some of same as he stood up. He didn't go all the way: he halted in a protective crouch.

Apple said, "Ah."

The man in the doorway remained silent and still. His rigidity, the spread of his feet, these gave word of his tension.

Telling himself not to be ashamed because he was

afraid, Apple removed a piece of lettuce from the front of his sweater and dropped it airily aside.

"I'm furious," he said. "Mad as hell." He gestured to the wall behind him. "I've walked along on top of that every night for a week. Like a tightrope, see. And I did it perfect. But tonight I have to go and fall off."

The man said nothing.

"I don't care that I could've done myself an injury," Apple went on. "I'm a steelworker, used to risk. What pisses me off is falling like a beginner. Oh well."

The man spoke. The language he used was French. He said, "Nice try, friend. But it won't wash."

"What's that?" Apple asked, bluffing back to what he felt sure could only be bluff on the man's part. "I didn't get it."

"Of course you did. In your profession, you have to know this language."

"If that's Eyetalian you're throwing at me—forget it. I don't know the lingo."

The man in the doorway switched to German: "I think that you had better come inside."

Apple said, "Now that one I do recognise. It's pig Latin. And you're telling me to get lost or you'll call the coppers. Is that right?"

Still in German: "Not badly done. You were taught the routine, I suppose, at Damian House."

That the KGB knew of the country mansion was no surprise to Apple, as the Brits knew about most of the places where Hammers and Sickles were trained.

He said, "Well, don't worry, I'm off. I've no intentions of hanging around in your stinking backyard." Turning, he stepped to the gate.

"This language you know," the man said in Russian, "if on the unlikely chance you don't know the others. Obviously, you wouldn't have been sent to pry and eavesdrop, or something worse, if you didn't understand the language of the house."

"What the bleeding hell're you rabbiting on about?" Apple asked, peering at the gate. It had no bolt, was locked by means of a key.

"So, friend, don't you think you should drop the act?"

There was a sound of movement from the doorway. It galvanised Apple into action. Almost before he had finished ordering himself to look lively and get on the ball and *move*, he had used the struts on the gate as steps and was clambering up onto the wall.

The man had come forwards into the yard, Apple saw on glancing aside. He looked away so that his gaze could help in the act of balancing as now he began to stand upright on the wall's apex.

Still using Russian, the man said, "Come back down. This is your last chance."

Apple stood in a tall crouch, an arm wavingly out at either side. His feet felt awkward. Not only were his shoes angled on the slope, but their soles were slippery from treading the garbage.

He took one step forwards, more slide than lift, then braved another. His body teetered to the right. He corrected with a wild seesawing of his arms.

"If you look back," the Russian said, still in his own language, "you will see that I am now holding a gun."

Apple couldn't look back even though he wanted to. For one thing, it would give away that he understood; for another, it would endanger his balance.

He said, with faked brightness, "I think I've got it."

"This gun," the man said, "is equipped with a silencer. No one will hear when I shoot you."

Apple took another step. "Yes, I'm doing fine."

"And shoot you is what I am going to do on the count of five," the man said. He added a slow, emphasised "One."

Apple longed to drop down to the alley and run, but then his bluff would be blown and possibly his part in the mission along with it. He could only hope that the shooting threat was also a bluff.

"Two."

His arms constantly dipping and rising like the bar on a scale, Apple went on along the wall. The slippery steps he took were mere inches long. It was more shuffle than walk.

He said, his voice a shade squeaky, "I've got it made."

The man said, "Three."

In a try at matching the brightness he was acting, Apple thought that at least if he did get killed it would be as a secret agent, not a linguist. He wouldn't go to some heavenly library, but to that great big keyhole in the sky.

"Four."

Apple shuffled on. He teetered not only sideways but back and forth as well. His arms swung, wheeled, jack-knifed and flapped. His knees quavered. His body jerked like someone with rapid hiccoughs.

The man said, "Five!"

Apple was unable to hold back his gasp of fear. He followed it at once with another, however, and then a third, which made the first seem to have been the beginning of a laugh.

He choked out, "I'm making it."

And there was no shot. There was no more of anything from the man in the yard. Apple began to laugh in nervous earnest. He let himself overbalance, and as he dropped to the alley he snorted, "Oh hell."

Apple rolled from the landing in the approved style. He got up, saw and heard nothing from behind and staggered off still giving nervous chuckles.

It was dark when he awoke from the dream. In it, he had been walking along the top of a fence, watched admiringly by Kate, who wore the clothes of an eight-year-old despite being her present-day height. The frilly dress failed to cover her panties.

Switching on the light, Apple looked at his watch. It was four o'clock in the morning. But he felt starkly awake. More, he felt stimulated. Whether this was because of the dream, or from his adventure with the Russian, or from frustration over Ethel, he didn't know. He did know he was in the mood for action.

After thinking for a minute, Apple got out of bed and started to dress quickly. Minutes later he was letting himself out of Harlequin Mansions.

At a sprightly pace he ran through Bloomsbury, down Charing Cross Road and along Shaftesbury Avenue. He stopped in Piccadilly Circus. Although the neons and bulbs above glared their commercial appeals, the area was void of human life.

Apple moved into the roadway. Sprinting, he ran in a wide circle around the centre island. He went around twice, shoulders back, head high. His eyes were unblinking and his smile was formed on closed lips.

Then he headed for home. He knew he would be able to sleep now.

At ten o'clock that same morning, Apple was in Spitalfields. It being Sunday, the only businesses open on the shopping mall were a newspaper kiosk and a snack bar. Apple tried the former first.

Out of habit when not in the country, he had put on his Sunday best. It was the first word in conformity, the last in drabness. He was well trained, Apple had thought sighingly after dressing. Where Pavlov's dogs salivated at the ring of a bell, so did Appleton Porter reach tamely for his Sunday best when London's belfries began to clamour.

At last Apple got to talk with the news vendor, an

older man with flickety eyes. He described the one he
sought in her Ms. Mayfair persona, since he felt that this
was sure to be closer to her true self than Mrs. Suburbia.

The news vendor looked Apple up and down. His eyes
said, "Copper," his mouth said, "Me, I don't know nobody. You wanna buy a paper?"

Apple bought three. Forgetfully, he left them in the
snack bar after having a cup of tea and getting another
negative response on Ms. Mayfair. Which reminded him
of Alexander Grishin and that today the wheelchair routine was going to be used.

And invalid who could afford a nurse would, naturally,
be dressed well, Apple mused. He congratulated himself
on having been shrewd enough to put on his Sunday
best.

Apple went in one of the residential towers. The
woman who opened the door called ADMINISTRATION
was friendly and talkative. She said she was a widow. She
said she liked tall men and them there scary movies
where you had to hold someone's hand. She said awful
things about everybody in the building, but couldn't say
there was anything familiar about the description of Ms.
Mayfair.

Feeling virtuous, Apple escaped. Over the following
hour he called not only on other administrators but also
made calls at randomly chosen flats in the four towers.
He drew a blank where he didn't rouse suspicion.

On an underground train heading west, Apple
thought that he would try the Mayfair beauty salon tomorrow. He daydreamed of uncovering a vast carnap
ring, its headquarters the salon. He would be a hero to
Kate. He would be on television. His picture would make
the front pages of all the newspapers. He would be fired
by Angus Watkin.

Snapping out of his daydream, Apple thought about

getting Ethel back safely and with no one knowing of the crisis except himself and Ms. Mayfair.

On a whim, having time to spare, Apple went from the station to the part of Kensington where he had parked Ethel on Friday. He thought there was a chance, slim but real, of finding the boy who had watched him drive away. That boy might have seen somebody else at the car minutes before.

There was no one on the Sunday street, young or old. Though Apple gave up on his whim, he lingered as long as possible because he felt here a connexion with Ethel. He had to run to reach Oranger Lane before noon.

Kate was waiting down a side street. Standing beside the Fiesta, she looked statuesquely beautiful in the white uniform of a nurse, her cap gleaming like a halo.

Thinking of angels, Apple stopped and said, "You look sensational."

She gave her quiet smile. "Thank you, Basil."

Apple made himself become businesslike. "Did anything happen last night?"

The smile turning rueful, Kate said, "Yes, it did. Flop happened. I dropped a clanger."

"You?"

"Happens to everybody, Basil."

"Of course it does," he said loyally, proudly and gratefully. "Our Alex put in an appearance after I left?"

"Yes, and I crawled behind him in the car. After a while he got a cab. I had it in neat sight for about ten minutes, then I got caught in a pocket of traffic. The taxi got away. I zipped around afterwards for a time, but no go."

Apple shook his head, spread his hands. "All my fault," he said. "Sorry."

"Your fault?"

"If we'd been twinning, as we ought to have been, it

wouldn't have happened. One of us could've tailed on foot, got a cab, hitched a ride, whatever."

"Well yes," Kate said. "I couldn't very well do that and ditch the car in traffic."

I would have, Apple thought, which obviously would have been the wrong move. "Certainly not," he said. "Me and my bloody headache."

"How is it, Basil? Forgive me for not asking sooner. You poor thing."

Craving more of the same, those pats and gazes of concern, Apple was tempted to say that he was still suffering but bearing up. Resisting, he said:

"Better, thank you. As a matter of fact, the pain went away soon after I got back to base. I took some aspirins."

Briskly and dismissingly, Kate said, "That's good."

"But it was murder while it lasted."

"Poor Basil."

Resisting again, Apple said, "So what I did was, I came back here."

"Really?"

He hadn't known until now that he was going to tell about last night. But he saw the sense in it, considered the decision wise of him. The incident might come to light later.

"I went around behind the house in case you were there," he said. "I got up onto the wall to see if you were in the yard, a man saw me and I left. That was all."

Kate nodded slowly, asking, "What man?"

"One from the overflow house."

"How well did he see you?"

"Not well at all," Apple said, shaking his head. "It was too dark there for details." Which was more or less true, he thought. Also, his constant crouch, below and above, would have disguised the fact of his unusual height.

"And you didn't learn anything?"

"Afraid not. It was flop all around."

"But we're still clean."

"It looks that way."

Brisk again, Kate snapped a look at her watch. It was so well done, efficient, nurselike that Apple almost put out his wrist for its pulse to be taken. This girl, he mused, is the tops.

Stepping towards the back of her black Fiesta, Kate said, "The wheelchair's folded up in here. We'd better get a move on."

While getting the chair out, Apple reflected on the weirdness of the espionage business. Within the space of a few hours, he had got himself soaking wet, had done a tightrope act along a wall, had nearly been shot at, had run through the predawn streets, had canvassed businesses and homes for information, had loitered in search of a small boy, and now was about to be pushed around in a wheelchair by a beautiful girl.

That only three out of the seven incidents were connected with the mission, Apple ignored. He was good at that, which he knew, but ignored that as well.

Alexander Grishin walked slowly in the pale sunshine. He seemed to have no particular aim. Over his hands, clasped behind, hung a raincoat. His manner was like that of many other Sunday strollers on the broad avenue.

Apple had his arms folded in an unconscious attempt to simulate that casualness. Another pose he knew about: he had his feet apart and his knees together in order to reduce the height of his lower legs.

For ten minutes now, ever since Grishin had come out of the overflow house, Apple had been a passenger in the chair. Secretly, he liked it. Being pushed by Kate was nice—the going no work for her—but particularly enjoyable were the glances of sympathy from passers-by.

At first Apple had assumed the expression of a person who was suffering from some obscure, romantic malaise, one you could mention anywhere. Later, because children weren't sharing in the sympathy but stared at him with dead eyes, he had decided that he wasn't an invalid after all; he had been in a dramatic accident—skiing, car racing, circus high wire.

Chin out, smile faintly cynical, Apple rolled along in comfort. Between glances at approaching strollers, he watched the man who was walking two hundred yards in front.

Another ten minutes passed before Alexander Grishin made a change in his line of action. Moving to the inside of the pavement, to a stone bench, he sat down after preparing his coat as a cushion.

Kate had brought the wheelchair to a halt. She went on again, but only a few yards, stopping by a kerbside postbox that was hidden from the bench ahead. The chair on wheels was mostly out of Grishin's sight.

Apple looked around as Kate was bending. They both asked, "What about the car?"

"Yes," Apple said, "you're right. We might need it."

"And we might have to go on doing this kind of shuttle."

"That's going to give you a lot of exercise."

"Lovely," Kate said. "Can you manage the propulsion wheels all right, if he goes on?"

"Like a champion."

For a while after Kate had gone, all that happened was that two separate people came up and asked if Apple wanted to be taken across the road. He declined with thanks.

Alexander Grishin got up. After stretching, he collected his raincoat, threw it over his left shoulder and walked on in the same amble as before.

Apple steered out from behind the postbox and began to propel himself forwards. He had made careful note of the business with the raincoat.

In the garment language that Apple had been taught, change of position meant the all-clear. There were eighty or so other set positions, each with a message for a colleague. But the code had been discontinued soon after Upstairs had bought from an unaligned spy the hat/garment/object code used by the Russians, who had discontinued it that same week, after they had bought the British code from the same spy.

Apple doubted, therefore, that Grishin was giving out signals, but would put all changes with the raincoat in his report anyway.

The Russian continued his stroll. He stayed on the same broad thoroughfare, where there were pockets of commerce among the private houses. Traffic was steady.

Apple stayed well back. Needing to be fully alert now that he was alone, he no longer sought balm in the eyes of strangers. He concentrated on keeping visual tabs on the man who went in and out of view beyond the intervening strollers, though with an occasional look behind for news of the Fiesta.

On turning back from one of these checks, Apple saw that Alexander Grishin had stopped. More, he was looking this way.

Apple put his head down and went on at the same easy speed. He steered gradually over to the kerb, where he halted by a group of people. He used them as cover.

The Russian was still looking back. The impression he gave was of being undecided about direction.

A red double-decker bus squealed and fumed to a stop beside the group of people, its open rear platform level with Apple's chair. The conductor jumped off.

Cheery-brusque, he said, "Let's go. I'm late."

With no cheer at all, a man in the queue threw back, "I'll say you are."

The next moment, Apple and his chair were being lifted onto the bus.

It happened quickly, with several people involved as well as the conductor. That Apple was unable to stop the transfer was due to a number of circumstances, in addition to his surprise.

The conductor was eager to meet his schedule; some of the people were late; some were trying to outdo others in a display of kindness; in the confusion of talk, questions, advice, Apple gave the right replies to the wrong enquirers:

When somebody asked if he was just waiting to meet someone and somebody else asked if he wanted to get on, he answered the first person with "No no, not at all." When others asked if they should take him off and somebody asked if he was going a long way, he answered that person with "Yes, please."

The wheelchair was bustled into the space under the stairs. Apple, his protests growing stronger as his surprise faded, made to rise. He hit his head on an understep and slammed back down again, gasping with pain.

The platform swiftly cleared of passengers, the conductor rang a bell, the bus started to move. Apple, one hand on top of his head, held the other out and said, "Listen. Wait."

"That's okay," the conductor said. "Have this ride on me." He hustled away into the body of the bus.

"Christ," Apple groaned.

The double-decker was picking up speed. It passed Alexander Grishin, who was now walking on again. He had his coat folded over his left arm. Apple noted automatically while telling himself he had to alight at the next stop, even if it meant getting up and carrying the chair. But that might be seen by the Russian.

Apple sat in a dready slump until there came a familiar squeal: brakes. The bus was slowing. Leaning forwards, craning up, Apple looked through the rear window. His surprise returned.

Alexander Grishin was running.

The bus came to a fast halt. Unsure whether to get off here or go on to the next stop, Apple sat taut, his hands gripping the propulsion wheels.

Two people got onto the platform and went inside. Grishin, mere yards away, was still running. Apple moved a hand to the front of his face. A bell rang. The vehicle jerked away.

Alexander Grishin, with a final burst of speed, reached the moving platform and jumped on.

Apple sank back. Through his fingers he watched as the Russian, who was no more than four feet away, stood looking through the back window.

"Keep the platform clear, please," the conductor chanted, coming out. Grishin went upstairs. The conductor followed.

Well well well, Apple thought. He wondered if, instinctively, he had guessed that Grishin was about to catch a bus and so had acted accordingly. Finding the idea stupid, he sadly let it go.

Apple looked through the rear window. Another minute passed before the black Fiesta appeared in the distance. It caught up quickly, Kate's head switching as she scanned for signs of twin and mark.

Apple looked into the body of the bus. No one was paying him any heed. He got up, stepped to the platform's back corner, grabbed the bar and leaned far out. Waving wildly, he got Kate's attention at once.

With more waves Apple explained the situation: he and chair were safely here, unrumbled, and Alexander Grishin was upstairs. Kate shook her head in admiration. Apple shrugged modestly.

The birdsong was so loud that it veered towards being unpretty, more cacophonous than musical. A constant shrilling, it came from every tree in the bird sanctuary's one hundred rolling acres.

Apple, appalled at the mere mental suggestion that he could find birdsong anything but charming, wore a fixed smile as Kate pushed him along under the arching branches.

It had been a long bus ride. The end had come with the conductor's call of "Terminus!" and Alexander Grishin's departure. Lifted to the ground by several willing hands, Apple had found himself beside the gate of the sanctuary, in which Grishin had been visible. Kate had soon come from parking her car.

Visible still was the Russian, among the trees, walking with his raincoat held behind him. Other strollers crisscrossed at all angles on the smooth grass. Every third person had a pair of binoculars.

Apple grew used to the birds' gossip as the shadowing went on. His light smile became natural—for his surroundings, for the girl behind who touched his shoulder occasionally as any good nurse would, for the fact of being on a mission.

Sometimes, Alexander Grishin would stride up a hillock and disappear down the other side. Reaching that point, Kate would make a detour rather than battle up the slope. The Russian was never out of sight for long.

Gradually, both the birdsong and the strollers lessened. Apple assumed that the feeding stations which brought the birds, which attracted the people, had been left behind.

Ahead, between wheelchair and mark, a man was leaning on a tree and using his binoculars to look around it. Familiar with this by now, Apple would have disregarded the man except for noticing that his binoculars were aimed downward, into a dip. On drawing level, he saw that the focal point wasn't a bird but a couple. The young man and girl, their clothes in copious disarray, were making love on the grass.

While swiftly, primly drawing Kate's attention to an imaginary bird in the opposite direction, Apple wondered if voyeurism was the real attraction here, and the reason for Grishin's visit. If, in fact, the behaviour which had aroused the interest of Upstairs was merely related to the Peeping Tom sport.

A minute later, Alexander Grishin went up and over another hillock. Kate quickened her pace. The side of the rise that she made for rose almost vertically, a baby butte.

When rounding this earthen wall Kate made a sudden, jerked halt. Apple nearly shot out of the chair. Grabbing on, he saw that Grishin was close at hand, sitting on a fallen tree.

Apple also saw, in the two seconds it took Kate to retreat unnoticed, that at the tree's far end sat a woman. Youngish, schoolmarmishly dressed, she had binoculars, two cameras, notebook and tape recorder.

Hidden by the wall, Apple and Kate conferred. Whispering, they agreed that, as the woman could be a contact, they had to try to get close, eavesdrop if not watch. The most obvious way was to play at romance, as they had before.

Kate said, "But even if he hasn't registered subconsciously the white uniform, and I don't think he has, is necking in the woods normal practice for an on-duty nurse?"

"Or for an invalid?" Apple asked. He was not, however, going to miss out on this opportunity. He said, "We'll ring the changes."

Hastily, Kate took off cap, dress and pumps, while Apple got out of his jacket. Clothing they stuffed in a satchel on the back of the wheelchair before pushing it close to the wall of earth. Kate now wore sweater and short skirt.

They went around to the slope. They climbed until the Russian's head came into view, then lay down on their faces. Settling, they listened. There was nothing to be heard.

Kate sneezed.

She and Apple turned on each other glares of alarm. Kate gasped, "The grass tickled my nose." On the heels of that came a thudding; it was felt in the ground, not heard.

Acting fast, with no finesse, Apple took Kate into his embrace. They lay side by side and cheek to cheek. Apple's head was the uppermost. Peering through a veil of fair hair, he saw the top half of a simian face appear on the hillcrest.

He murmured this to Kate, adding, "Let's make it look good." He kissed her on the lips.

Kate responded like a pro. She moved her head gently, she stroked his neck and shoulder, she returned the probe and pressure of his mouth.

After a moment, Apple remembered the mark. He relaxed the kiss to peer upwards. Alexander Grishin had gone.

Kate murmured, "Still there?"

Apple mumbled, "Yes."

"The show must go on."

"We need more realism," Apple got in before returning his mouth to Kate's. He next put his hand on one of her breasts. It, he decided, had character. It was lenient on the surface but with an underlining firmness; it had benevolence and body and the correct degree of overall wobble.

Kate gave a realistic sigh. She ran her caress from the nape of Apple's neck to his arm and then on down to the small of his back.

Like a good pupil, Apple also lowered his hand. He placed it on Kate's hip, which seemed to meet it with gentle gusto. After a squeezing linger there, he moved on lower yet, down a leg.

Kate whispered through the kiss, "Is he still there?"

Following a slight upwards movement with his head, Apple said, "Yes." He forgave himself for the lies with a munificence that he couldn't help but admire, which emotion swamped his guilt at lying.

His hand came to the skirt's hem. It slipped neatly underneath onto the naked thigh and began to insinuate its way upwards, moving in slow strokes.

Kate swallowed loudly.

The wandering hand climbed apace. As it went, it pincered on and off the taut, quivering thigh muscle. It was in no hurry, but nevertheless came at last to a silkiness of undergarment. The thumb dithered.

Kate performed a passionate jostle, during which her head went back. Becoming still, she said, "He's gone."

Apple asked a drowsy, "Who?"

Kate disentangled herself and got up. She crouched higher on the slope, turned and reported, "He's moved on. Let's go." She hurried towards the chair.

Apple was slower to react. Feeling a little stiff, he got up slowly. As he did so, his sweep of gaze caught glimpses of four pairs of binoculars retreating around four separate trees.

He didn't know whose idea it was to switch roles in respect of the wheelchair. He was hardly aware of the decision to do an image change until, his mind clearing, he found himself pushing Kate away from the butte. Their clothing they had left as was.

Glancing back, Apple saw that the woman was still sitting on the fallen tree. He wondered about her. He wondered further if one of the phony bird watchers was a double phony—if he or she could be an Angus Watkin twins-watcher.

The Russian, his coat looped about his neck, was well ahead, walking with less dawdle than before. He also went in a straight line as opposed to his previous tacking.

It was Apple who tacked. The terrain being mostly uphill, he tried to make the going easier for himself by taking oblique lines. It was still hard work. Kate was a large girl. Smiling gamely, Apple pushed and sweated and thought how wise of him not to have put his jacket on again.

The land continued climbing. Leaving the I-spy entirely to Kate, Apple moved in a stoop, head down, arms straight, legs bent for leverage. He panted like a dog.

When Apple heard Kate hiss at him to stop, he sank gratefully to his knees. Looking around, Kate said there was no need to hide. She added, "Our Alex is busy."

Swallowing a whimper, Apple pulled himself upright. He saw that they were on the edge of a clearing. In it were rustic tables and chairs, a coffee stall, a brick-built lavatory with doors labelled NYMPHS and SHEPHERDS and a telephone kiosk.

Two or three people sat at the tables, a youth was using the telephone. Alexander Grishin, faced the other way, stood at the coffee-stall counter talking to its attendant, a teenage girl.

"She's out of it," Kate said. "Too young."

Panting, Apple nodded.

"Bet you what you like, Basil, that telephone's the reason he's here."

Apple managed a sickly, "Yes."

"How about if I try Routine 7—if he does use the blower? I think it might work."

What "Routine 7" was Apple didn't know. He put his head on one side as though in consideration, which served as an answer and saved him having to use breath to speak.

"Got some change, Basil?"

He gave her all the coins in his pocket. She moved off at a dawdle, her goal apparently to circle around the glade. Thankfully, Apple sat in the wheelchair.

Some minutes later, the youth came out of the telephone box. At once, Alexander Grishin left his cup on the counter, strode to the kiosk and entered. Within seconds of that, Kate hurried inwards from the glade's edge.

Grishin had the receiver to his face. By the movements of his head, he had just made a connexion, was talking, when Kate arrived there. She rapped smartly on the door. Snatching the receiver down, Grishin put a hand over its mouthpiece and eased the door open with his elbow.

Faintly but clearly Apple heard ninety percent of the exchange, meaning the part which came from Kate. The while shaking coins in cupped hands, she said in a commanding manner that she had an important call to make. She was late for tea at a friend's house. Just how long was he going to be? She couldn't stand around here all day. Some people seemd to think they could monopolise public telephones for hours.

Appearing to be unruffled, Alexander Grishin bowed slightly and let the door close. He took his hand off the mouthpiece as he turned the other way.

Kate didn't move off. After the haughty performance she had put on, it would have looked odd if she did. Even unsmitten, Apple would have been impressed.

Grishin kept his call brief, though Apple doubted if he had been influenced by Kate. Her act, however, could have been a flop, Routine 7 no mystery to the Russian.

Alexander Grishin came out of the box. Bowing, he held the door for Kate (who flounced inside without sparing him a glance) and then went off out of sight beyond the coffee stall.

Kate's pretend call was also brief. Leaving the kiosk

she came over the grass at a stride. Her eyes were shining with triumph and pride.

Bending, slapping the chair arms, she said, "Our Alex has fixed a rendezvous. He's meeting some person, name unknown, at the Brand Hotel, room 314, on Tuesday at eight o'clock."

"That's great," Apple said. "You're a genius."

"I got lucky."

"I hope it isn't a Red's herring."

Kate shook her head emphatically. "When he went back to his call, he said in Russian that he'd had to break off because of some stupid woman, but that it was pretty funny because there was a spider in her hair."

"Standard trick."

"I know. I didn't make a move. So he went on and set up this meeting for the day after tomorrow."

"Could it be a woman? I mean something that wouldn't be of interest to us?"

"Male or female I couldn't say, and I don't know if our Alex was giving orders or taking them, but it was definitely a business arrangement."

Apple smiled. He said, "Seems to me we're making progress."

"But meanwhile, let's stick to the trail."

They looked around. The Russian was nowhere in sight. Apple got up unwillingly. His legs still felt like unwatered rubber plants.

He said, "We'll take a big detour around the glade. I'll go this way. Meet you at the other side."

They separated, leaving the wheelchair. Apple went at a pace to pacify his legs. He saw nothing. Meeting Kate again, he agreed with her that they had probably lost the mark.

"But let's keep strolling along in this direction," Kate said. "Just in case."

"Right. While we talk about this meeting on Tuesday night. Do we call in, report it?"

"I wasn't given any instructions in that respect."

"Nor I," Apple said. "So we play it as we see fit."

"Precisely."

"Okay—how?"

They thought about it. Apple suggested they try to get the next room, 315, and hope to hear what was going on through the wall.

Kate was enthusiatic. She said, "But to get that room we'll need a good story and a good image. An expensive image. In any case, we'll want to ring the changes again by then."

"Listen," Apple said, feeling clever. "If our Alex isn't aware of the tallness by now, he might get to be. Right?"

"Absolutely."

"We can't shrink, but we *can* make ourselves taller still, and at the same time put on the rich bit for the hotel."

"How?"

"We go as Texans."

"Beautiful," Kate said. "High-heel boots and Stetson hats a foot tall. You're a genuis."

"I got lucky."

Still strolling, they discussed details. They had just decided on which theatrical costumers to go to when a voice snapped, "There they are."

There was a man. There was a woman. Both were over average height and sturdily built, both were fair and pink-faced and about thirty, both wore casual clothes and every hint of the middle-middle-class. And both bristled, as if someone had accused them of having socialistic tendencies.

It was the woman who had spoken. As Apple and Kate

came to a stop, she spoke again: "You thought you'd got away with it, didn't you?"

The man added, "Well, you have another think coming."

They moved forwards until the two couples were standing close, man to man and woman to woman. The strangers folded their arms like mothers on the doorstep.

Kate asked in a bemused tone, "What on earth are you two talking about?"

"As if you didn't know," the woman snorted. Her friend said, "You must think we're idiots."

Apple stopped being surprised. He took Kate's elbow between finger and thumb and rapidly squeezed out in Morse, twice each to be sure, the letters *H* and *S.*

While the woman's British accent was perfect, the man's was less so. It might have fooled a thousand people, including old star pros, but it didn't fool Appleton Porter. He knew that the man had spent most of his life in Leningrad.

All signs pointed to the couple being a Hammer and Sickle. It also seemed clear that, whatever their aim might be, they weren't sure if Apple and Kate were spooks or straight.

The woman had been talking. It was slowly coming through that Apple and Kate were being accused of having covertly watched the couple making love.

Apple interrupted. He blustered, "But this is ludicrous! Isn't it, Cynthia? We're respectable married people. We don't *do* things like that."

The woman said, "She's not wearing a wedding ring."

Kate: "We don't believe in such things."

"I knew it. Bloody radicals."

Kate gasped, Apple told the woman to have the goodness to watch her language, she told him to go to hell, and the man began a tirade against filthy Peeping Toms.

Soon the woman joined in. Apple and Kate started to

argue back, protesting their innocence and counter-charging paranoia, alcoholism, feeble-mindedness and gross vanity in not wearing spectacles.

Included in the exchange were snippets of biographical information. Somehow, both sides managed to get in personal details. Names were followed by mention of the office and the gallery, Chelsea and Norwood, the Rolls and the children, Cannes and Brighton, war bonds and a wound pension, ex-Navy and civil defence.

Apple began to see the absurdity of it all. We suspect them of being spooks, he thought, and they suspect us. The longer this goes on, the more obvious will it be that the suspicions all around are correct—ordinary people would either have come to blows by now or have stalked off.

The couple had been growing more animated and belligerent. They snarled and gesticulated like hellfire preachers.

"Careful," Apple warned. "We've been taking karate lessons. Right, Cynthia?"

"Yes, Gordon," Kate said. "I'm glad we did now. These idiots are probably muggers."

"Maybe we should go to the police."

"We should. Come on."

"Oh no you don't," the man said. He made a grab for Apple and his companion did the same towards Kate.

The fight was on.

For a moment, all was a jumble of shouts and skirmish, of grabs and slaps and pushes. The couple, Apple knew, were going to have a difficult time prevailing at unarmed combat while making it appear as if they knew nothing about it.

Apple took a punch in the belly. Oofing, he staggered back. The little strength that was left in his legs from pushing the chair, it fled. He sat with a bump.

The woman snatched hold of Kate's right arm, the

man took her left. Whatever it was they planned, it didn't come off. After lunging forwards between them, Kate whipped back and swung her arms together. The couple crashed heads.

They relaxed their holds and weaved aside. Kate flung herself at the man. She hit him in the face with a Queensberry left, thunked him in the groin with a Limehouse right. He fell.

Apple had got up. Weakly, he went towards the woman. She, closing the gap rapidly, swung a high kick. It was beautifully done. Had Apple been of normal height, he would have taken it on the chin. Instead, he got it in the chest.

His breath oofed out again. He sloped forwards like a falling telegraph pole. Ducking, the woman took him across her shoulder in fireman style. She straightened with a violent jerk. Apple flipped up in the air and came down with a crash on his back.

Dazed, hurting everywhere, he rolled over just as a kick whizzed by his ear. He pushed up to his knees, deflected another kick, and in doing so knocked the woman off balance.

Kate had the man by one leg. She was turning in a fast circle, swinging her opponent as if he were a child being given a thrill. Twisting, he rose and fell in swoops. Twice his head and shoulders bounced off the ground with an ugly thud.

Getting up, Apple closed with the woman. She hit him with three judo chops in quick succession: neck, biceps, ribs. His one return blow went over her head.

Kate let go of the man. He went sailing away through space, wheeling like a windmill. A tree came in useful. The man slammed against it. Dropping to the ground, he lay still.

Kate, meanwhile, had fallen. She had lost her balance after the twirling.

Apple threw another slicing blow. The woman grabbed his arm and twisted underneath. The preventive action he knew how to take he couldn't, because of weakness and pain.

His feet left the ground. He met it again with his head, but managed enough of a roll to minimise damage. Even so, he felt that he was finished.

His roll ending with him on his hands and knees, Apple was in time to see the woman coming at him. The position of her arms showed that she was about to kick. Apple doubted if he could move.

At the last second Kate arrived. Her body a blur of speed, she hit with a rugby tackle. The woman cried out and shot aside. She kept her balance—until Kate, following, reversing her horizontal flight path, smashed her in the face with both feet.

The woman was unconscious before she hit the grass, obviously: her landing had a drunk's deadness. Her friend by the tree was stirring, with groans.

Grabbing Apple's arm, Kate hauled him to his feet. She said, "Come on, Gordon. We'd better report these mad brutes."

Apple mumbled, trying to get control over his reluctant legs and foggy mind.

Kate half led, half carried him away, still talking about brutes and muggers and police. Not until they were well out of earshot did she drop the act.

She asked worriedly, "Are you all right, Basil?"

"A bit battered," Apple said, his brain clearing. "I dare say I'll survive. With help."

"Were we convincing, d'you think?"

"More so than they were. Though it's still not definite that they're KGB."

"In my view they are," Kate said. "But look. If our Alex is a nonentity, why would a Hammer and Sickle be running interference for him?"

"Maybe they weren't. Maybe they're as interested in knowing what he's up to as we are."

Kate got him into the wheelchair. She fussed, attentive and sympathetic. He didn't mind giving in to his pain with whimpers, which became more frequent once the chair was in motion, being pushed at a jiggling speed over the grass.

They reached the car without seeing any of the Russians. After helping Apple on with his coat, Kate put the chair inside. She mentioned that she happened to be a 10 in unarmed combat. Apple gave his true 5 as a 9 and said he would be glad when he got completely over that bout of influenza.

Driving, Kate said, "You're going to be as sore as a boil in the morning. So tell you what. I'll do the A.M. watch on our Alex. Okay?"

"You, Kate, are terrific. If they only had medals in this racket."

"Nonsense. We'll meet midafternoon, say three, at the costumer's."

"Right," Apple said. "And if anything spicy develops beforehand, give me a call."

Kate nodded. "But for this moment in time, as the politicos say, shall I put you in a cab when we get to town?"

Apple, cunning: "I don't know if I can manage alone. You maybe had better take me back to my base, if you don't mind."

"That's terribly irregular," Kate said. "So naturally I'll be glad to."

During the rest of the journey they held an inquest on their morning's work. The verdict was that it had been a total success, if only in respect of finding out about Alexander Grishin's meeting on Tuesday at eight.

At Harlequin Mansions, Kate helped Apple out of her

car, inside and up to the flat. For the first time, Apple regretted the lack of a lift.

"A hot bath straight away," Kate said. "That's what you need for those abused muscles."

"Yes, nurse."

In the bathroom, after easing down into a chair, Apple gazed up and said plaintively, "I don't know if I'll be able to undress myself."

Kate fingered her chin thoughtfully. "Oh."

"Not without a great deal of pain."

"I see."

"Agony."

"Yes."

The telephone rang. Kate said the telephone was ringing and Apple said somebody must have dialled the wrong number, no one ever called him here.

"Not even Upstairs, Basil?"

"Well, yes. But not at this hour. Forget it."

"No, I'd best answer," Kate said. "Where's the phone?"

Sighing, Apple told her. She was gone less than a minute. Stopping in the doorway, Kate said with a hint of coolness in her light smile, "A woman. Sexy voice. Wants to talk to a Mr. Porter. I'll forget that name immediately. She's holding on."

"Okay. I'll be right there."

"Ask the lady to come and help you," Kate said, leaving. "See you at Galdoni's tomorrow. 'Bye."

Forgetting intriguing and erotic possibilities such as two-in-a-bath and find-the-sponge, Apple got up and creaked through to the living room. He lifted the receiver. As expected, the caller was Ms. Mayfair.

Apple told her curtly, "You didn't show up last night."

"Of course not," the disguised voice said. "We are not exactly beginners in this business, you know."

"What're you talking about?"

"You had the police with you."

Apple shook his head—once—stopping when his neck twinged with pain. "No, I didn't. I was alone."

"They were in a taxi around the corner."

"Rubbish. There was only the driver in that cab."

"Mr. Porter," the woman said, "it is well known that the police have a taxi which they use for undercover operations. They call it Myrtle or something like that."

Apple would have laughed at the incredibility of it all if it hadn't also been so frustrating. He asked, "Did you get the cab's number?"

"Yes."

"Then check on it. You'll find that it was a genuine taxi. The police are *not* in on this. I've told no one."

"Very well, we will check," the woman said. "Assuming you to be telling the truth, the transfer of money can take place tomorrow night, at eight. Same place."

"Fine. I'll be there. Alone."

After a short pause, the woman said, "But come to think of it, tomorrow is out. This is our busy time just now. Make it the day after. Tuesday night at eight o'clock. Good-bye."

CHAPTER 3

Having gone to sleep before it was dark, Apple awoke before it was light. Notwithstanding the fact that he had been in bed for twelve hours, he stayed on there, pampering himself. He felt cozy. His aches and pains were quite bearable, and even enjoyable, resulting as they did from incidents in an espionage operation.

Apple relived the events of yesterday, with repeat returns to his mock-serious necking session with Kate. Recalling the blow on his head while under the bus staircase, he stroked carefully into his hair and was positive he could feel a lump. He dwelled on how shrewd of him it had been with the couple to allay suspicion by underplaying his skill at unarmed combat. He remembered how close Kate had come to helping him undress.

Which reminded Apple of Ms. Mayfair. After another fume at the annoying coincidence of Tuesday at eight, he wondered if this delaying and non-showing was intentional, a tactic. It might go on and on, the idea being to tease the victim into paying an exorbitant sum in ransom.

Apple decided not to worry about that until after Tuesday. And in respect of the rendezvous, the big problem was how he would manage to be both at Primrose Hill and the Brand Hotel.

Apple was still playing with ways and means when he fell asleep again.

Awake at nine, he got up and put on his robe. He

moved around gently, feeling the wounded veteran. His breakfast was a tough one of coffee and cigarettes.

Holding in his lips another cigarette—unlit, for the smoke would otherwise get in his eyes—Apple sat at the writing desk to add yesterday to his report. He kept the wording short, curt, as though this were the kind of thing he did every day and it was all rather a bore. But he typed slowly to make it last.

At ten o'clock Apple looked in the telephone directory, found the Mayfair beauty salon and dialled its number. To the answering voice he explained about seeing from a bus this lady leaving the shop on Saturday morning. She could be his long-lost cousin, who was due to inherit part of the family millions.

After he had given a description, the voice said it was familiar but only because it fitted about seventy percent of the customers and that in any case there had been no one in the salon on Saturday except interior decorators.

Gently pacing in the living room, again missing Monico's support at this time of crisis, Apple mulled over the situation with Ethel. He supposed that it was naïve of him to put all his trust in the carnappers. Tuesday could become Thursday, then Sunday, then a week hence; and Ethel meanwhile, if teasing for a bigger ransom wasn't the game, could be on her way to where such entities were valued highly, perhaps South America.

Apple concluded that he ought to double his efforts to find Ethel himself. Apart from another visit to Spitalfields, however, what else could he do?

Firmly, Apple went to the kitchen. He cut slices of brown bread, he plugged in the toaster, he put the kettle on to boil. Within five minutes he was sitting at the table with tea and toast, the latter heavily coated with lemon marmalade. This formed not only his favourite snack but also his most effective food for thought.

Apple sipped and crunched slowly. Not forcing his

mind to its task, he allowed it to wander. He felt euphoric, almost in a state of trance.

The idea came when he was midway through his second slice. He snapped alert. He chewed busily and drank his tea in gulps, the while nodding in self-congratulation.

Licking his fingers, Apple headed for the writing desk to get his little grey book. It contained the telephone numbers of his friends.

Like Apple himself, most of his friends were a little out of the ordinary. With some it was physical. The majority, however, were convinced, as was Apple, that their real potential had never been seen by the powers that be but had no right to be, as evidenced by their blindness. Gold was there for the mining, the friends knew as surely as they had never known success in their chosen fields. Life was treating them if not shabbily, then with a definite measure of fray.

Typical was Ogden Renfrew. A white-haired handsome man close to seventy, he had spent fifty of those years nearly being discovered. He was an actor. Between long bouts of resting he had briefly carried spears, asked if there was anyone for tennis or announced that dinner was served. When he did find work nowadays, it was as a voice, dubbing English in the sound tracks of foreign movies.

Although Apple's friends were, of course, important to him at all times, they were particularly so this morning because of the fact that few of them had regular employment. They were, therefore, available.

Apple searched through his little grey book avidly. He was thinking in terms of address more than person. After jotting down numbers for a while, he went to the telephone to start making calls.

The pub, down a back street in unglamorous Southwark, was called the Bellringer Arms, as its first landlord had been head ringer at Southwark Cathedral, which could be seen from the top part of a window in a back room.

The Bellringer's present landlord, Alf, was merely a manager. He worked for a company which owned nationwide a hundred hostelries, from humble pub to plush hotel. Alf aspired to plushness. He couldn't understand why the company didn't put him in charge of one of its West End palaces.

It was Alf whom Apple saw first when he entered the pub at noon. The landlord, plump and forty, greeted his friend in a stream of wet Cockney. It would have been unintelligible were it not for the profanity, which rang out with precision.

Crackling his earwax in forgiveness, Apple followed Alf to the back room where other friends waited. They hailed him with cheer or josh, according to kind.

Maude said in warning, "You've gained weight." She was a thin soprano whose voice had the paleness that comes from permanent dieting.

"You look great, kid," Duke Ellington said. A jazz pianist whose gigs were mainly limited to the Bellringer Arms, Duke refused to use any other name than that which he had legally acquired by deed poll. He was a Jamaican, as dark as deep purple.

Ogden Renfrew, with a throwaway line from a play he was almost connected with once as understudy to the juvenile lead, pulled Apple down onto a chair at the large table.

He asked, "What's the strife, lad?"

Others echoed the question. Carolina Winterdale-Moore said in her refined way that she hoped it wasn't something quite dreadful. Patsy, an ex-girlfriend of Apple's, said he was probably in love again, the poor lamb. John Blake advised that they all wait until Apple had made a statement.

"Yes," Jim Hall said. "All belt up." Jim was a grossly fat man who made people nervous; no one that size had any right to be so swift and agile.

Apple held up a hand. "First," he said, "let me buy a round of drinks. What'll it be?"

While the drinks were being brought by a barmaid in answer to a shout from Alf, Apple talked to the man at his side. Jock Ward, swarthy as a Sicilian brigand, was a sometime auctioneer. Apple was always fascinated by the skill Jock used to avoid words that revealed his lisp.

Drinks served, Ogden Renfrew said, "You're on, lad."

Apple began by saying that they all knew Ethel, which brought fond smiles and queries as to her well-being.

"She's fine, I hope," Apple said. "I wouldn't know. She's gone."

John Blake stood up from among the murmurers. An ex-policeman, he was six feet two, bald and stout. He had retired recently from thirty years of remaining a constable.

He asked gruffly, "Lost, stolen or strayed?"

"Nothing like that, John."

"We'll need a photograph, of course. And a fingerprint outfit might come in handy."

Apple shook his head. "Let me explain," he said. "It's my colleagues at the Institute. I made a foolish bet with them. I said that Ethel was so distinctive that if she were anywhere in London I could find her within forty-eight hours."

Jim Hall said, "Forty-eight minutes, more like."

"That's what I thought. But after the bet was made, a couple of hours ago, I realised my mistake. I was assuming, you see, that they'd park her on a street somewhere."

"Of course," John Blake said, sitting. "In an area designated for parking purposes."

Apple said, "But there's nothing in the rules to stop

them putting Ethel out of sight. Which, they told me happily, is exactly what they're going to do."

Carolina Winterdale-Moore gasped. Her gaunt, imperious, middle-aged face trembled in rigidity. She opened and closed one hand while saying, "The pigs. The rotten dogs. They should have their legs cut from under them."

"Come now, Carolina."

"I mean it, Apple. At the least they deserve to have their teeth knocked down their cunning throats."

Jock Ward asked carefully, "What might be won or not won in the outcome of your wager?"

"Holidays. They'll take mine if I lose, and I'll stand in for them at the Institute. Too bad if it happens. I was going to show Monico the Highlands."

Everyone responded suitably. Alf reeled off a string of Anglo-Saxonisms. Others groaned or hissed. Ogden Renfrew quoted Lear. Carolina Winterdale-Moore said wait till she told her associates at the Pacifist League.

"I mustn't lose that bet," Apple said. "That's why I asked you all to meet me here. I want your advice." He slapped his knees and got up. "I want you to tell me the best way to go about finding Ethel. So think about it, please."

Turning away, he strolled to the end window, leaving behind him a growing swell of talk. Although he knew that it was possible for one of the group to come up with an idea that hadn't occurred to him, he doubted it. He was backing on them finding the same solution that he had found with his toast and marmalade.

The nine people were from different districts of London. If they searched there and got their local friends to help, poking into alleys and yards, public and private garages, old buildings and regular parking lots, they might very well discover where Ethel was being hidden.

He himself would nose about in Bloomsbury, Apple

thought. It would be a clever move on the carnappers' part to hide Ethel right on his own doorstep.

Apple further thought that he had been sensible in not giving the group his idea straight out. It was too big a favour to ask, coming cold. If it came from them and was shared, it would take on a different character.

Cheerfully, feeling that success was just around the corner, Apple gazed out of the window. That he had lied to his friends didn't bother him, as it was temporary. He would tell them the truth once he had Ethel safely home.

Looking at Southwark Cathedral, Apple reminded himself not to mention that John Harvard, founder of the American college, had been baptised there when it had been simply St. Saviour's Church. They had heard that one before.

Apple's ex-girlfriend came over to him from the arguing group. Patsy, twenty-five, was a professional beauty queen, though the only title she had ever won was Miss Tooting East (four times). She had an incredibly voluptuous body and the face of a boxer.

Patsy said, "We can't seem to agree. My idea's dead fab but no one likes it 'cept me."

"What is it?"

"You put an item in the papers, see, in the personal column. You offer a reward."

"No time for that, Patsy."

"Well, there's Carolina's idea. She thinks Duke and big Jim ought to go and get your colleagues and beat the daylights out of 'em."

"That would be cheating."

They were joined by the ex-policeman, who said, "I've got the answer, Apple. You get leaflets printed. About three million should do it. You hire a small plane and you scatter them all over London."

"That, John, might take too long."

"Really? What a shame."

Ogden Renfrew, tossing back his long white hair, came over and said grandly, "An appeal. That's the solution. I go on television tonight after the news and make an impassioned appeal for help."

"Balls," Alf said, coming up behind the actor. "They don't do that stuff on the telly no more."

"Perchance you have a better idea?"

"Yes. What we do is, we contact every villain in London. They'll find old Eth in no time flat."

John Blake said, "There will be no consorting with the criminal element, the scum of the underworld."

The landlord told him, "Watch it, you. Them's me mates you're talking about."

Duke Ellington and the fat man led Carolina Winterdale-Moore over. All speaking together, they said they had agreed that the answer was not to beat up the colleagues. Jim Hall added, "We get just one of them and threaten to torture him until he tells us of Ethel's location."

John Blake said that wouldn't be sporting; leaflets would. Maude, arriving with the auctioneer, said thinly that Apple should go back to the Institute and beg for mercy.

Jock Ward suggested, "We hire a van with a hailer on top. I, being driven around, give out the pertinent information and offer a liberal remuneration for help."

The others derided the plan and began to lobby for their own suggestions. This, Apple thought, could go on for hours. Matters had to be hurried along.

After a glance around the group, Apple called out, smiling, "Yes, that's it." His friends falling silent, he said, "Thank you. It's a wonderful idea."

Someone asked, "Whose was it?"

"Quite so," Apple said. "And I know it's going to work, because, as it happens, by coincidence, purely by accident, each one of you is from a different part of the city."

Apple spent an hour asking about Ms. Mayfair in Spitalfields, where he had a sandwich lunch, an hour snooping around the hidden crannies of Bloomsbury. He discovered nothing. Still cheerful about Ethel, about everything, he went to Soho.

Galdoni's had been there forever, it was said. The firm had rented Lady Godiva her G-string, had outfitted the Cavaliers and had supplied royal wigs to the bald crowned heads of Europe. Apple suspected exaggeration.

He did know, however, that Galdoni's was where the Secret Services turned first if their own Dress Departments were unable to supply the needed.

A nondescript doorway led to a dim labyrinth of rooms, halls and passageways. There was a mothball tang in the air. On every side, and in many places dangling from above, were garments. No division of style, type or period was in evidence.

A dummy in black came alive and asked if it could be of service. Apple said he was meeting someone; they were interested in cowboy outfits. The shadow took him along tunnels to a clothing-choked cavern.

With a disarming smile, Apple said he ought to have brought his canary with him to test for gas fumes. The shadow, not amused, left.

Apple began to browse. He looked doubtfully along the racks. Everything was spangles and fringes, stars and glitter, fine for *Annie Get Your Gun* but too much for the Brand Hotel.

Even so, Apple was intrigued. His doubt turned to longing. He could imagine himself striding along a busy London thoroughfare in ten-gallon hat, purple shirt with white piping, striped pants and high-heel boots.

Apple was reaching for a buckskin jacket, telling himself he could at least try the thing on, when he heard footsteps. Turning, he saw Kate enter the cavern.

He greeted her with a hurried, "Hello. These're all pretty wild. My rating is a 5 in unarmed combat. I think we'll want something a little less vivid. Some of these colours would stun a rainbow."

Kate blinked. "Well yes," she said. "But what a shame. They're so gorgeous."

Apple lifted the sleeve of a spangled garment. "You'd look fabulous in this deal, for instance. But you'd stop the traffic."

"And all we want to do is impress a hotel employee."

"About that."

Strolling beside the racks, they discussed the Brand. A plan of approach agreed on, they further agreed that, because of the meeting in room 314, Alexander Grishin would hardly be up to other intrigues tomorrow, therefore they would give the I-spy a miss until evening at the hotel.

"In fact, this morning was a dead loss," Kate said. "A waste of time."

"Tonight I'll do the watch," Apple said, "to make up for you slaving away alone while I groaned abed with my wounds." He waited for sympathy.

Kate touched his arm. "Sorry, I forgot to ask. How are you feeling, Basil?"

Apple, not unusually, outclevered himself. He said, "Oh, I'm fine. It was nothing, nothing at all."

"Good," Kate said in brisk dismissal. "And thanks for doing my bit this evening. I want to wash my hair."

Not caring to know about things like that, about there being everyday domestic doings in the lives of pro espionage agents, Apple said equally briskly, "I'll call you tomorrow about a rendezvous time."

"Fine. Now before I forget."

Kate produced a small object, which she dropped into

Apple's palm. "A cigarette end," she said. "I found it yesterday when we split up to circle that glade. It was in the path that our Alex had taken."

Apple looked closely at the inch-long tube. The paper was brown, the filter black. He nodded with recognition. "Yes, it's Russian."

"I thought so. But isn't it a rare type?"

"Yes. Rare and of course expensive. Your Ivan in the street doesn't smoke these, any more than he can get a ticket for the Bolshoi."

"Reserved for big-noise Party people?"

"Precisely," Apple said. He went on to tell of seeing the cigarettes in Paris once, when he had acted as interpretor at a Soviet-British bargaining session over the exchange of imprisoned spies. He tried to make the tedious, overlong session sound glamorous.

At one point, his gaze roving as he talked, Apple saw a flash of movement in a corner of the dim cavern. Though he wouldn't have sworn to it, he had the impression that what had caused the flash was a man with a beard.

"The question is," Kate said when Apple had finished, "how come lowly Alex has a supply of the near unobtainable?"

"And here, in Britain, at that."

"But, naturally, the cigarette could've been dropped by someone else."

"True. Have we seen Alex smoking?"

Kate shrugged. "I'm ashamed to say I don't remember."

"Neither do I," Apple said. "Smoking's one of those acts that're so common you don't see it." He put the butt end in his pocket. "But to the matter of clothes."

They gave their attention back to the racks, browsing and shaking their heads. In a moment, his voice lowered, Apple asked casually, "By the way, did you see someone else here a while ago?"

Kate, playing her fingers along a fringe, said a flat "No, I didn't."

"Must've been mistaken," Apple mumbled, glad he had played it casual. He reminded himself not to overdo the mystery bit, which was the mark of an amateur. In any case, every fourth man in London had a beard.

Browsing on, they came to the conclusion, Apple reluctantly, that all they would need for their impersonation of Texan tourists was boots and hats, which they could wear with the denims they already owned.

Within half an hour, business transacted, Apple and Kate were leaving Galdoni's. They separated on the street. Apple strolled alone to Shaftesbury Avenue. He carried a large black Stetson in one hand, in the other a paper sack containing a pair of high-heel cowboy boots.

Apple had a feeling of disappointment. It was as if he had been let down on a promise. That the promise, or near promise, had been made to him by himself was beside the point. He still felt vaguely abused.

Apple didn't pause to question his action some minutes later, when he found that he was walking into a store. He merely noted that it was the gentlemen's outfitters which he had often patronised in the past.

Not slowing, he went straight to the stairs, where a sign said OUTSIZE DEPT. He strode upwards firmly.

Now he knew why he was here and what it was he wanted. The item was one he had yearned for ever since becoming a part of the Intelligence machine. But he had never dared acquire it out of fear of exciting derision among colleagues, exasperation Upstairs. The item was too obvious. It was too celebrated a part of fiction, fable and joke in connexion with espionage. As was a kilt to a comic-opera Scotsman, so was the item to a cartoon spook.

A salesman approached. Calmly, Apple told him, "I'd like to see something in trench coats, please."

Closing the flat door behind him, Apple slapped the black Stetson onto a peg of the hatstand, dropped the bagged boots aside and strode through to his bedroom. With fingers that weren't quite steady he began to unfasten the parcel.

The aroma arose as Apple folded back the paper: that bouquet of freshness which belonged inside pastry shops and showroom cars, by flower stalls and mountain streams, and to all new garments.

Apple lifted the trench coat gently by the collar, watching it unfold. He hadn't tried it on in the shop, only asking—out of experience—for the largest size, and then requesting that the hem be let down to its fullest, which had been done while he waited.

He put the coat on now. It was an excellent fit, he thought, looking at himself in the full-length mirror, though perhaps a little too broad across the shoulders. He tied the belt—the buckle should never be used—and tugged the various folds into slight disarray. Slowly, smiling, he turned this way and that to see his reflection from every angle.

At length, sated for the time being with visual effects, Apple wandered around the flat. He sat and leaned. He smoked a cigarette. Some of his ash he let fall on the coat.

Apple still kept his trench coat on while preparing and eating a snack of coffee and a fried-egg sandwich. Only when it was time to shower did he remove the new garment, which, after putting it carefully onto a hanger, he carried to the hatstand. Backing off like a courtier, he went into the bathroom.

During his shower, because of guilt, Apple thought exclusively about Ethel. Although he had hopes that his friends might locate her before tomorrow evening, he toyed again with ideas for playing a double game—Brand Hotel and Primrose Hill. He came up with a solution that he thought might just work if he were nimble enough.

It was after that, drying off, that Apple realised he would not, of course, wear the trench coat tonight, or at any other time in connexion with the mission. He had known it all along, just as surely as he knew that ridicule was the strongest weapon. He might be seen by someone, meaning an operation watcher, possibly that bearded man who may not be a figment of his love of intrigue.

Slightly low in spirits at having again let himself down in a promise which he hadn't completely made in the first place, Apple dressed in a dull suit with tie to match, put on a scarf and quickly left the flat.

He went up in spirits again presently, when passing the railings in front of the British Museum. Because of ideas formulated in that grey building by a German over a century ago, he mused, an Englishman was having to stalk a Russian through a London twilight.

Apple went to the Tottenham Court Road underground station, where he boarded a train, packed at exodus hour. He stood among swaying commuters and wondered smugly what they would think if only they knew who he was.

Leaving the train at Notting Hill Gate, Apple went out to the main road. He was confident of Alexander Grishin coming this way. Within sight of the Soviet Embassy he took up the watch from the opposite side of the bustling thoroughfare.

In his element, Apple strolled and loitered, smoked a cigarette, casually checked his watch, yawned, crossed to the other side of the road and came back again.

Alexander Grishin appeared. After a short pause he began to walk west, as expected. He had no coat.

It was almost dark now and the overhead lights were on in all their glare. Apple sauntered away to a patch of dimness. Turning there, he saw that the Russian had already drawn level; that, in fact, he was walking at a good clip.

Staying on his own side of the road, Apple kept almost abreast. He was pleased and intrigued by what could be untypical haste on Alexander Grishin's part. Certainly, thus far during the mission he had never moved with such speed.

At short length, the Russian reached Oranger Lane and went into the overflow house. Once more Apple started going through all the standard ploys of the stationary I-spy.

An hour passed pleasantly.

Reappearing, wearing now a bow tie but still without a coat, the mark walked off in the opposite direction. Apple followed. He decided that he had been wrong about garment signals but gave consideration to that natty bow tie.

Moving at the same clip as earlier, Alexander Grishin walked only five or six short streets. The last of these was lined with grubby businesses, all now closed. Midway along, the mark seemed to vanish.

Apple approached the fade stage with caution. This could be a trap. Perhaps the Russian, seeing that he had only half of the tail which he had become aware of some time ago, had concluded that this was a safe time to act. There was no one else on the street.

With ten yards left to cover, Apple stopped. There were several orthodox gambits he could use. The trouble with them all was that if they failed it meant at best being rumbled, at worst a bullet in the head.

Apple chose the unorthodox. Falling into a crouch like a mime doing burglar, he moved along on tiptoe, his knees lifting high. He had no idea what, if he was seen, the mark would make of him; he did know he didn't look like an espionage agent on active service.

Apple came level with the fade stage. It was deserted. Stopping, straightening, he looked at the only direction that Alexander Grishin could have taken: a doorway, lighted dimly, with above it a faint red sign saying Caveman Club.

Not wasting time on debating the proper procedure, Apple moved to and through the doorway. Stairs went down in scruffy narrowness from the sill. Twisting his scarf to semi-hide his lower face, Apple began to descend. He allowed his shoes to thud on the cracked linoleum.

Below, a passage stretched away from a man sitting at a table. Neatly dressed and sharp of feature, he bore a vague resemblance to Fashion-plate at Earl's Court. He was reading a paperback.

Not looking up, he said as Apple stopped at the table, "Members only."

"I'm new in the district."

"Non-members can only be admitted if guests of a bona fide member, who must pay one pound for said guest." He looked up. "I'm a member."

"Thank you," Apple said. He brought out a pound note and put it on the table.

Looking back down at his book, the man said blandly, "Go on in, guest."

A place of entertainment that calls itself a club should, to give satisfaction, be either glamorous or sleazy; be either a whirl of mink, champagne and beautiful people or a stagger of apache caps, rum and razor scars. Anything in between—cozy, seedy, friendly—is bound to be a disappointment.

Apple, however, refused to be disappointed. He saw the mundane cellar as squalid, its male element as sinister and its female as sluttish. So, being for Apple sleazy, the Caveman was glamorous.

Plastic cloths covered the twenty or thirty tables that stood around the brick pillars. A bandstand held an upright piano, beer crates and a sign saying there was live music every Fri and Sat. A bar stretched along one side. Decor was blank wall or hand-lettered posters relating to pizza, dart matches, raffles, garage sales, bingo on Wed.

Halting himself from continuing his scan, which could rouse suspicion, Apple moved to the bar and sat on a stool. Sole server, a skeletal man in shirt sleeves, asked what it would be then. Apple, noting the plethora of beer bottles, ordered a light ale.

Not until he had been served, had sipped and felt that he was no longer being looked at with interest did Apple turn to the side and scan on.

Present were fifty-odd people, a quarter of them female. Most sat drinking at tables, with a handful strewn out along the bar. The men were a mixed lot, ranging in kind from one in paint-speckled coveralls to a pair of well-dressed executive types, ranging in age from early twenties to sixties.

It was different with the women. Without exception, they were young and attractive, overly made-up and flashy of dress. Where the men could be anything, the women could only be B-girls, Apple knew. He told himself he had been right about the club in the first place.

One of the girls, a blonde, stood beside the table at which Alexander Grishin was sitting alone. They were talking. In profile to Apple, the Russian was doing most of the listening. His attitude seemed to be one of politeness. From time to time he shook his head.

After another minute of this, the blonde touched Grishin's shoulder and drifted away. She went with rolling hips to where another girl posed against a pillar.

Apple sipped his beer. He thought it unlikely that the girl was a contact of some kind, but that if she was, the meeting had been smoothly done.

As Apple was lowering the glass, and with his other hand tugging his scarf back up into place, he saw that the blonde was approaching. He tensed.

Stopping beside him, leaning an elbow on the bar, the girl said, "Hello, soldier."

"Good evening."

"Care to buy a lady a drink?"

Apple hesitated. On the one hand, keeping the girl here would be good camouflage; on the other, he might need to make a fast departure if Grishin left.

"Sorry," Apple said, his smile regretful. "It just so happens that I'm waiting for someone."

The girl swung her hips. "Maybe she won't show up."

Meaningfully: "As a matter of fact, I hope she doesn't."

In a hackneyed drone: "I knew you were a devil as soon as I saw you."

"Right. I'm even worse than old Jimmy there." With a slant of his head he indicated Alexander Grishin.

"Who?"

"The man you were just talking to. It's Jimmy Stamp, isn't it, who works at the betting shop?"

The girl shrugged. "Calls himself Carl around here. Maybe that's phony, which wouldn't be anything new. Or maybe you made a mistake."

Apple nodded. "I did. Now that I see him clearly, he's not Jimmy."

Bored, the blonde touched his shoulder and moved on. "See you around, soldier."

Apple congratulated himself. He had established that the Russian was a regular at the Caveman Club and that he used a different name.

Time passed. People arrived and left. Two girls danced together to the jukebox music. Alexander Grishin, finishing his beer, had the skeletal bartender bring him another. Apple felt obliged to do the same, rather than draw attention to himself by lingering too long over one drink. He burped behind the scarf.

A new girl came in. She was like the others in every respect save one. Where they were slender, she was generously built, though voluptuous withal, a normal waist dividing heavy breasts from heavier hips.

She walked straight to where Alexander Grishin was sitting. He got up at once. A smile on his simian face, he shook hands with the girl and ushered her into a chair, bent over her in query, straightened, signalled for service and sat down.

Apple, observing as closely as he dared, couldn't make up his mind if the two were well acquainted or were meeting for the first time. A certain formality in Grishin's manner seemed to suggest the latter, though he might simply be a formal person, not unusual for his nationality.

The girl was less reserved, smiling and talking with some animation. Aged about twenty-five, she had a cute face that was small in comparison to the girth below. She wore a clinging dress. Her cosmetics were expertly applied. She had straight black hair cut in the style of a Japanese doll. Apple decided that she could be of almost any Western culture, though he gave her the code-name of Geisha.

Again time passed. The couple talked on casually— Apple failing in his several tries at lipreading. Alexander Grishin stayed with his second beer even though the girl had a repeat: gin and tonic. Geisha smoked several cigarettes and each time offered her packet to the Russian, who always declined. Nothing changed hands. There was no touching above or below the table. There was no mannerism that could be suspected of covering signals.

Apple was on the point of ordering, reluctantly, another beer, prompted by sour looks from the barman, when Alexander Grishin got up. After shaking hands with Geisha, he turned away and walked to the exit.

Apple followed one minute later. At the foot of the stairs, pausing by the slick-dressed man who was still reading, he asked, "Was that Carl I just saw leaving?"

Absently, engrossed: "Who?"

Apple went on up. Out in the street, he saw his mark rounding the corner. He hurried. This he repeated until Grishin went from sight for the last time, into the overflow house.

Apple lingered in Oranger Lane for a quarter hour. The I-spy was less enjoyable now because he had a feeling of urgency, as well as being a little light-headed from the two beers.

Alexander Grishin had gone to ground for the night, Apple concluded. He set off back for the Caveman Club.

"Members only."

"I came out a little while ago."

"I've heard that one before."

"You must remember me."

Eyes on his book, the man chanted, "Non-members can only be admitted if guests of a bona fide member, who must pay one pound for said guest." He glanced up. "I'm a member."

"So is Carl," Apple said. "I'm his guest tonight."

The man said, "Don't know any Carl, and he'd have to be here anyway."

Apple brought out money, from which he selected the dirtiest pound note. He put it on the table with a sarcastic "Most kind of you to oblige."

"Go on in, guest."

The scene inside had changed slightly. There were a dozen or so more people, and three couples were dancing on the space on front of the bandstand.

One of the dancers was Geisha. That she was half a

head taller than her middle-aged partner gave Apple a perverse satisfaction. Pulling his scarf down jauntily, he went to the bar, where he raised a finger.

The barman came. "Beer, sir?"

"No, thank you. A sherry on the rocks, please. La Ina, if you have it."

"Never even heard of it. Nor that combination. Sounds rotten. Wouldn't you like a nice lager?"

Apple insisted on his order. By the time this exchange was over, the music had stopped. Glancing around, Apple saw that Geisha had separated from her partner. She was standing with the blonde and another girl. They appeared to be boredly chatting.

Apple's drink came. After paying, he turned on his stool and leaned back on the bar. He noted that Geisha's gaze, slowly sweeping around, was about to reach him. When it did, he raised his glass in a sophisticated gesture. He thought it came off rather well.

Geisha hadn't noticed. Her gaze swept on by. Apple smiled to show himself that he wasn't perturbed, swallowed half his sherry and tinkled the ice in the glass with a practiced wrist dither.

The music started again. Two couples got up to dance. The blonde, Geisha and another girl—they began a sort of three-way shuffle. Apple, nodding to the beat, sipped away the rest of his sherry.

The tune ended. Another one started as soon as the dancers, tired of waiting, had moved away. Geisha strolled around the side of the room.

Bold in drink, Apple put down his glass and left the stool. He went straight across to the ample girl, who stopped on seeing his aim. She looked at him with curiosity.

Apple asked, "Would you care to dance?"

The look, now directed upwards, turned to doubt. She

said, "I don't think so, thanks." The accent was English provincial.

"I've been told I'm a bit on the tall side."

"Well, you are a bit, yes."

"Okay, so instead of dancing, how about if I buy you a drink?"

"That'd be nice," Geisha said. She had a friendly, natural mien. "I'll have a double g-and-t, please."

They sat at a nearby table. Without being told, the barman brought a sherry on the rocks and a gin and tonic. He asked Geisha, "How's tricks, kid?"

The girl said, "One at a time, Tim." When the thin man had gone she told Apple, "My name's Anne."

"I'm John."

She laughed abruptly. "You're as funny as Tim."

Although he didn't quite get the joke, Apple was pleased. He felt witty, debonair, urbane. If it hadn't been for the mission, which he remembered in time, he would have related this humorous anecdote he had heard recently about a spelling confusion in Latin.

"Cheers, John or whatever."

"Cheers, Anne."

They sipped their drinks. Idly, Geisha talked of a movie she had seen on television. Apple found her likeable. He thought it too bad that she needed to work as a B-girl, con for highly priced drinks that were actually only water.

So Apple was pleased and surprised when, presently, he had an opportunity to test her drink. He dipped it with a fingertip, which he then tasted. The gin and tonic was genuine.

Geisha lit another cigarette. Apple was about to start on a build-up to the subject of Carl/Grishin, when the girl asked, "Well, how about it?"

"Another drink? Certainly." He drained his glass.

"No, thanks. I've had plenty for now."

"Tell the truth, so've I."

"Good," Geisha said. "So let's talk prices."

Apple said he didn't understand much about inflation, which made his companion frown. He said, "Sorry."

Geisha leaned forwards. "Listen. You didn't buy me a drink just for a conversation, did you?"

"Well . . ."

"You don't want to talk about your domestic problems, do you?"

"What? Oh no."

"I mean, I don't have a lot of time to waste. The pubs'll be closing in about two hours."

Apple didn't know what she was talking about. He told himself he ought to have known better than to have had that last drink.

Still in her forward lean, still frowning, Geisha said, "You do realise that I'm a business girl, don't you?"

"Everyone works nowadays," Apple said comfortingly. "What line are you in, Anne?"

The girl looked at him steadily. Her frown faded. With a light smile she said, "The oldest in the world, actually."

Apple returned the steady look. He gave a long slow nod on a long slow "Oh."

Leaning back and patting her fringe, Geisha began to talk brightly of the routine that she and the other girls followed, to avoid the now-illegal streetwalking. The Caveman and other clubs were where they could meet new clients and regulars, pubs were where they angled for tourists.

His discomfort fading, Apple went back to feeling urbane. The Caveman had become much sleazier.

"I bet your name really is John," the girl said.

"Yes, it is."

"And I bet you've got a girlfriend."

"I have, yes, sort of."

Geisha stubbed her cigarette. "Ah well. I'd best be

moving on. There's the rent to earn." She stood up. "Thanks for the drink."

"Wait," Apple said, again remembering the mission. "Wait a minute."

The girl returned to her seat briskly. "Ten pounds for a short time, thirty quid the night."

Stoutly, Apple said, "And very reasonable too."

"Eh? You mean you're not going to try and bargain?"

Apple almost blushed at such an audacious notion. "Of course not."

Geisha shook her head as ponderously as though she had a tender neck. "Hey," she said. "Hello, John."

"Hello, Anne."

"Listen. What if we say twenty-five for the all-nighter?"

Apple countered, "What if we say fifteen pounds for the short-timer?"

"Hey, you're terrific."

And you are talkative, Apple thought, so long as you're not in a hurry. He asked, "Shall we go?"

It was five minutes away, a house that had seen worse days as an Edwardian tenement. Now, its recent coating of stucco painted white, it was a bride to medium chic.

The flat was a single, large room. One corner had been walled off to make a bathroom, another was a kitchenette, a third held the bed and the last acted as living area. There, on a couch, Apple sat himself to recover from his unsteady climb up several flights of stairs.

"Drop of Scotch, John?" Geisha asked. Not hearing the gasped negative, she went to a cupboard. She hummed like a housewife after spring cleaning.

Telling himself he could get rid of the drink somehow, just as he would manage to avoid going through with the coition, Apple got out three five-pound notes. He put them on a side table, discreetly, all but hidden under an ashtray.

The floor trembled as Geisha came across. She was carrying a glass. By a flick of her eyes followed by a nod, she established and acknowledged the money's presence. She heeled off her shoes. Stocking tops flashed briefly under her dress as she stepped up onto the couch. She knelt beside Apple.

"This Scotch is twelve years old," she said, "and it couldn't be going to a nicer resting place."

"We'll share it, mm?"

"Oh, I'll have a dram or two to keep you company." She put an arm around Apple and brought the glass to his mouth, serving him as if he were a child.

Serving me as if I were a potentate, Apple thought, and she my handmaiden. He sipped, swallowed. Since he found the taste unpleasant, he wondered if there could be a drug in the drink. It was an exciting idea. But it fled when Geisha herself took from the glass what Apple could see was a genuine draught.

She licked her lips. "Like it, John?"

"Delicious," he said gamely.

"Well, let's finish it off," Geisha said. "The rest of it's all yours." She returned the glass to his mouth.

There was no way he could get out of drinking, Apple realised, without offending the girl. Accepting the whisky, he gulped and gagged. He rolled his eyes as if in appreciation, which made the room swirl.

Leaving him gasping, Geisha took the empty glass from his mouth and put it behind the couch, at the same time switching off a lamp there. The lighting was drastically reduced.

"That man you were . . ." Apple began, but drooled off as Geisha, with a single swift hand movement, unfastened a dozen buttons at the top of her dress. It came open to the waist. The next movement was equally proficient, though performed at a reverse velocity. Apple's vision became slowly filled with two mammoth breasts.

They came closer. Trembling like hungry predators, they separated in their approach.

Geisha pressed Apple's head to her bosom. Apple found himself becoming aroused. Only distantly was he aware of being edged sideways and down. Soon he was lying obliquely on the couch seat, his feet on the floor.

Geisha straddled him and expertly dealt with the various barriers of clothing.

"This is nice," Geisha murmured. "I could stay like this for hours."

Wheezing in air, Apple said, "Carl."

"What, dear?"

"Carl. Saw him at club. Out of prison."

Hair scuffled under Apple's chin as the large girl shook her head. "You've got the wrong man, dear."

"Not a crook?"

Again the scuffle of hair. "And he definitely hasn't been in stir. I've seen him a couple of times a week for months."

"Friend of yours?" Apple asked, tightly, like someone carrying a sack of cement.

"Sort of. Businesswise."

"Looks foreign."

"No, not my Carl. He's as English as old muffins. Speaks educated, like you."

Apple wondered if they were, in fact, talking about two different people. He also wondered how much longer he could stand bearing the weight of Geisha's body. But he daren't break the cozy, chatty spell by asking her to move. He whimpered.

"What's that, dear?"

"Carl."

"Funny, but someone else was asking me about him not long ago. Can't remember who."

"Carl's been here?"

"Yes. He visits me every Thursday. Other times we have a drink together at the Caveman. He's nice, like you. Maybe you're both in the same trade."

After drawing in a long, painful breath, Apple said, "Why was someone asking questions about him?"

"Search me. Anyway, I didn't say a word. He's probably married, though I wouldn't know. He never talks about himself."

"Could be a crook."

"No, I can smell both crooks and cops, me."

"That someone with questions. Did he come here?"

Geisha scuffled hair against his chin. "No. The only one connected with Carl that ever came here was a mate of his. It was a little emergency of some kind."

"Oh?" Apple said. His left leg was going to sleep.

"They acted it up. Carl pretended to be angry and this man pretended to be like his inferior. They went out in the hall to talk. As Carl came in again I heard the man call him 'comrade.' "

"Still acting it up, of course."

"Oh no. That was real, I could tell. In fact, it was from that that I figured Carl out."

Apple said, "Ah." But he was having to concentrate hard in order to stay interested. The alcohol had him woozy, his leg was beginning to mortify, his lungs were being flattened.

Geisha said, "Carl belongs to a trade union, that's what it is, and his rivals for his top position're trying to get something on him."

"Could be," Apple managed.

Geisha thumped his chin up and down with firm nods. "I'd be willing to bet on it."

"Get what kind of something?"

"That he's cheating on his wife with a business girl."

Apple, near the end of his endurance, grunted. Geisha

said, "If it wasn't that you have nice eyes, I'd think you were one of his rivals as well."

The laugh that Apple tried, it made his squashed lungs revolt in a spasm of pain. He croaked.

Geisha asked, "What's that, dear?"

Apple whispered, "I have to go."

He was walking along a main road, keeping a lookout for a vacant taxi. He walked unsteadily, because of the alcohol and the lingering pins and needles in his left leg. He was also exhausted from his crushing on the couch and related activities.

But Apple felt as up as could be. He felt debauched, an habitué of low dives, a star drinking man, altogether a real pro. In respect of Kate, he felt the underhand two-timing bastard who in reality he could never hope to be. He felt wonderful.

Also, Apple reminded himself, he had cleverly wormed out of Anne, seductive daughter of joy, several provocative items of information, which would be mulled over at leisure. It had been, all in all, an extremely productive evening, the cost of which would be borne by Upstairs.

Apple's leg had recovered by the time he flagged down a passing cab. He wore a jaded expression while getting in, used a hard voice to give his address, over-tipped outrageously at Harlequin Mansions.

Apple swayed his way up three staircases. Turning onto his own hall, he almost overbalanced, which he ignored with eyebrows disdainful.

He unlocked his door, pushed it open, stepped inside. Then his heart stopped. At the same second he switched on the light, he saw the man.

The man was behind the door.

Half a second later, Apple was reacting.

He flung up a protective arm and threw himself in the

other direction. It was a strong throw for such a short distance. He hit the wall with a mighty crash.

Most of that impact Apple took on his shoulder and the side of his face. Dazed, he slid down to a kneel. One arm was still raised. Beyond it, he saw that the man was not a man.

The figure, held up by the hatstand, was formed by his new trench coat topped by the Stetson hat.

Apple began to blush. It was a three-alarm attack. The heat came rushing from somewhere in the region of his armpits, prickled his chest, concentrated itself to surge up his neck, and then spattered onto his face like scalding water from a burst pipe.

Apple didn't need to see himself to know he was the colour of a tomato that had reached the throw-away stage. He got up weakly. After slapping the door closed behind him, he moved away—mainly to leave the scene of his shame.

In the living room he collapsed into a chair and began on his latest short-term cure.

Apple pursed his lips in a whistle shape. Next he bulged out his cheeks. Third he put a clenched hand to his mouth as does a burper. Last he started to blow air strenuously into his fist.

The advertiser claimed that if you were pretending to blow up a balloon, one which was on the point of bursting, the effort plus the change of mental direction plus the fear of the imminent explosion would drive the blush into retreat.

This was Apple's first try with the cure. He was relieved to find that it was working, and quickly. He thought it might even last him for several months.

The blush pinked its way down. Apple straightened his features and lowered his hand. Feeling wetness on one cheek, he assumed that the red attack had been so strong it had made his eyes water.

He touched the place, looked at his finger, saw blood. The telephone rang.

Feeling now a throbbing ache in his right eyebrow, which, he realised, he must have cut in hitting the wall, Apple clamped a handkerchief there while going to the corner table.

The caller was Ogden Renfrew. He said, "Tried to get you several times this evening, lad."

"You have news of Ethel?"

"No, but I thought you'd like to know that I'm out there seeking. Therefore, be not dismayed."

Apple said he wouldn't, thanked the actor and rang off. He hurried to the bathroom, where he looked in the mirror to examine his wound. About an inch long, but not deep, it was bleeding gently. He was bending to the tap when the telephone rang again.

The caller was Duke Ellington, who said he had tried getting through several times. "But no answer."

"Have you found Ethel?"

The pianist said he hadn't, he was only calling to say that he hadn't given up the search. As before, Apple's disappointment was tempered by the fact that he was calmly talking on the telephone while blood was running down his face.

Apple thanked Duke and disconnected. Back in the bathroom, he had stemmed the bleeding by the time the next, expected call came. It was Carolina Winterdale-Moore, who, she said, had tried several times to get through this evening.

"But you haven't found Ethel."

"No, but I looked outside and on the car park between bouts. I'm at the all-in wrestling."

After disconnecting, Apple stood on beside the table. A full minute passed before the telephone rang. Smiling fondly, Apple picked up the receiver and said, "I know, you've tried several times to get me."

There was a pause. It ended with a voice saying "No, Porter, I certainly have not." It was the voice of Angus Watkin.

Apple straightened. "Sorry, sir. I thought you were someone else."

Ignoring that, his Control said, "I tried to contact you only once, a minute and a half ago, after I had reached this region."

"This region, sir?"

"Bloomsbury," Angus Watkin said, making the place sound like a flooded slum. "The area in which you reside."

"I see, sir."

"You do not, of course. But myself you will see. Be down on the street in five minutes, please." The line clicked to silence.

Apple stepped outside. He looked at cars. None that he could see into clearly had passengers. He looked both ways along the pavement.

Each side had one person coming in this direction. One was a youngish man carrying a bulging pillowcase. The other was an older woman who seemed to be having a conversation with herself.

She was the closest. Apple watched her come on, heard her snap "Rubbish" as she drew level, turned with her and watched her walk away.

The man was near now. "Catch," he called, and threw the pillowcase, which Apple managed to catch despite his surprise. Passing, the man said, "Follow me, please."

Apple obeyed. He stayed four paces behind. Glancing in the untied mouth of the bundle, he saw that it held dirty laundry. He asked, quietly but carryingly, "What's all this about?"

"Bit of stage dressing," the man said with his head

turned to the side. He was average in every way. "You must be the tallest man in London."

"Nowhere near. The tallest is about a foot more than me."

"Christ. Poor bastard."

They crossed the road, turned a corner, went along another street. Late now, there were few people about, and of the business establishments ahead only one had a blaze of light as opposed to token illumination.

On reaching that point, the man in front said, "There you go. So long."

"See you," Apple said. He went into the laundromat. It was long and narrow. There were machines on either hand, a row of chairs down the middle. At the front a young couple sat holding hands, at the rear sat Angus Watkin.

Apple walked to the back. "Good evening, sir."

His Control nodded. "Take a seat, Porter. You may discard your burden."

While tossing the pillowcase aside and sitting, Apple acknowledged Watkin's logic in not asking his underling to bring laundry of his own: that would have given away type of destination.

"We have been in the wars, I see, Porter."

Apple touched his face near the cut. "It's nothing, sir."

"I am less concerned about your physical condition than about the mission. One trusts that you are not aggravating matters."

"It happened at home."

"Also," Angus Watkin said, "you smell strongly of alcohol."

"I only had a couple of drinks, sir."

The nearby machine which had been humming merrily chugged into silence. Watkin rose, leaned forwards, put a coin in the slot and pressed a button. The hum started again.

Back in his chair, which was next to Apple's, Angus Watkin ordered, "Progress report, please."

Apple began with Earl's Court and the man he had named Fashion-plate. He continued until he saw that his chief was drumming one finger.

"But perhaps, sir, you'd prefer to wait and read my written report. It has more detail than I can give you from memory."

"And said report is, no doubt, on its way to me by post."

This was a Watkin joke. Smiling politely, Apple said, "No, sir. It's at home."

"Whereabouts exactly? Let me see if I can guess. Would it, mayhap, be in your typewriter?"

Apple wondered how much of a guess that was. "Yes, sir."

Betraying no emotion, although, as his underling knew, that was about the only thing he would not betray, apart from his country and Upstairs, Angus Watkin said, "Then I suggest, Porter, that when you return home you extract the report from your typewriter and put it in a safe place, one of those in which you received wise instruction during your training days."

Apple, quietly: "Yes, sir."

Watkin went on to lecture languidly about battles being lost through the loss of a horseshoe nail. He mentioned burglars, nosy neighbours, maintenance people and children out for adventure or vandalism. He broke off when the door of the laundromat opened.

A man of about thirty got as far as the threshold. He halted there with a jerk, which matched in time the jerk that took Apple, when the young couple suddenly became animated.

The girl snapped, "Pig!"

Her companion snarled, "I'm just warning you

straight. The next time you even look at another guy I'm going to kick the tripes out of you."

The man retreated, his gaze down, and closed the door. The young couple subsided. Watkin people, Apple accepted.

His chief asked, mildly, "Where was I?" He knew, but wanted to know if Apple knew.

"You were castigating me, sir, for my gross stupidity in having left a report in full view."

"Ah well. All agents are imperfect."

As had happened occasionally in the past, Apple suspected Angus Watkin of being part human. Which he took back at once when the older man added, "But some agents are more imperfect than others."

"Quite, sir."

"If I may paraphrase Tolstoy."

Apple was aware that his chief knew the author in question to be George Orwell, but wondered if he knew that his real name had been Eric Blair. He decided not to mention it.

"Be that as it may," Angus Watkin said, "let us get on to the nub, the reason for my presence here. To wit, your activities this evening."

"Yes, sir," Apple said. He cleared his throat. "At six o'clock I picked up the mark on Bayswater Road and . . ."

"No, Porter. The activities I refer to are those following the return of Alexander Grishin to the overflow house."

"Oh."

"In fine, when you went back to the Caveman Club."

Apple acted an understated gape. "I was followed?"

"Of course not," Watkin said. "I don't have people to spare for that kind of nonsense. I'm not the CIA."

Toadying, Apple crinkled his eyes to show that he

shared his chief's dislike of the Mayflowers. He wished he hadn't. His cut eyebrow hurt.

"I do, however, have one of my people in the Caveman," Angus Watkin said. "Let me tell you what you did tonight."

While he was doing so—accurately—Apple worked out that the agent was probably the blonde, whom he had asked about Grishin/Carl. She had tried hard to get friendly with the Russian tonight. So: the tailing twins weren't the only ones on this little errand.

Angus Watkin ended with "You were told quite clearly, if memory serves me right, not to get involved and not to go sidetracking."

"I've never been close to the mark, sir."

"True. Very true. But you did sidetrack."

"I, sir?"

"You, sir," Angus Watkin said. "You went with a girl called Anne. The same girl who had been talking to Grishin."

"That was Romansh. I mean, romance."

As though musing aloud, Watkin asked, "Only a couple of drinks?"

"And I don't even mean that," Apple said. "I mean sex." He became urgent, seeing himself being pulled out of the mission. "After all, the mark had gone to ground, as I judged the situation, so I felt free to take some off-duty time."

"Sex, I believe you said."

Nodding, Apple played a trump. "I admit to having been stimulated somewhat by my twin, Kate. But non-fraternisation is the rule, and I would never, ever break that rule. Tonight, therefore, I went with a prostitute."

After a bland pause, Angus Watkin asked, "You didn't question this Anne person about the man she had been talking to earlier?"

"No, sir. I don't believe in disobeying orders. It's a principle of mine.

Watkin gave one of his sighs. In almost anyone else it would have been a weary moan. He turned to look at the clothes whirling around in the washer.

Hoping this was dismissal, Apple asked, "Is there anything else, sir?"

Angus Watkin told the machine "I received information, which isn't firm, that you were seen in Soho today."

"I was there, sir, yes."

"Carrying a large cowboy hat?"

Knowing it was useless to lie: "Yes, sir."

Watkin looked around. "How you do surprise me, Porter."

That'll be the day, Apple thought. He said, "It's for a fancy-dress party I'm going to next week."

"Just so long as you don't let it interfere with your more worthwhile activities."

"Indeed, sir."

Angus Watkin moved one elbow forwards and back. "That is all, Porter. You may go."

Apple got up. "Thank you, sir."

"Oh, one last thing."

"Sir?"

From the breast pocket of his average suit Angus Watkin brought out a small fold of money. He said, "Here are the two pounds which you paid to get into the Caveman Club. Good night, Porter."

Apple trudged homeward through the quiet nighttime streets of Bloomsbury. He felt exhausted. The alcohol inside him had died, leaving in its wake a funereal heaviness of his spirits, a grave heaviness in his stomach, a coffin bleakness in his mouth.

Apple told himself he ought to have suspected the doorman. Also, he wouldn't now be able to get his fifteen pounds back from Accounts, having told Angus bloody Watkin that his doings with Anne had been strictly personal.

That made Apple feel greedy. He shifted away by thinking of how well he had handled his Control, who had possibly been intent on pulling him out. So, wherever else he may not have shone, he was still in the game.

Apple came at length to Harlequin Mansions. He went in by the large, impressive front door. As he reached aside with his left hand to swing the door closed, he thought he glimpsed there a man.

With a derisive laugh Apple turned fully that way, at which moment the man, who was real, threw a punch. It crashed onto Apple's jaw and sent him flying across the hallway and on into darkness.

CHAPTER 4

Apple turned up the collar of his trench coat. Although the sky was cloudless, he mused, March in Britain was notorious for its treachery, so rain could come pouring down without a moment's notice. Best to be prepared.

Severe of face, Apple walked on along Fleet Street. The centre of the press world was midday busy, bustling with both foot and wheeled traffic. Few pedestrians ignored the tall man who went striding by.

Apple was aware of that. It was some minutes before he found, in the entryway of a store, a spot where he felt unobserved. He looked at his reflection in the window.

It definitely added something, Apple thought, having the collar turned up. Especially with that cut on the eyebrow and that blue lump beside the chin. All the picture needed was a smouldering, lip-held cigarette.

People came out of the store. Apple moved off to continue his aimless walk around the City, which, he had concluded, was the best way to cure a hangover.

He lit a cigarette and felt perfect, felt he represented what was only the truth: an Intelligence operative who had been battered in the line of duty and who would later be meeting a beautiful lady spy.

Apple even took pleasure in the twinge of pain that came now when, in removing the cigarette from his lips, he nudged the bruise on his chin.

Last night, Apple had become conscious, to find himself on the floor of the hallway. That he was alive surprised him, when he had got all his faculties back. Nor had he been attacked after the initial blow. He assumed that his key had been taken—and returned—so his attacker could gain entry to his apartment.

However, on staggering upstairs Apple had discovered nothing amiss in the flat. Neither had there been that creepy sensation that an intruder often leaves behind. The typewriter still held his report, which Apple then took out, folded up small and placed in full view under the leg of a coffee table. Then he had gone to bed.

Apple discarded his cigarette by flicking it away into the gutter. He thought about his attacker. All that had drawn his attention respecting detail was the fact that the man owned a beard—a full, dark growth. He felt sure that Beaver, as he now code-named him, was the man he had seen before on several occasions throughout the mission. This was more gut reaction than sight identification, plus the circumstantial evidence of coincidence carrying itself too far.

But whether or not Beaver was the sometime shadow, what was the reason for the punch that seemed to have had no follow-up? It was, of course, possible for the man to have been in the flat without leaving physical proof or a sensation spoor, especially if he were a pro. On the other hand, a man who could gain entry through the house door, which was always locked, would have little trouble with the door of the apartment. Therefore . . .

Apple's hangover headache was growing stronger. He left the subject for the present, acknowledging only that Beaver was certainly not one of Watkin's people.

After having his third black coffee of the morning in a snack bar, Apple went in a telephone booth, whose door he held open with a foot because of his claustrophobia. He dialled Kate's number. She answered on the second ring.

"About tonight," Apple said, greetings over. "What if

we meet at seven, by the Roosevelt statue in Grosvenor Square."

"That's ideal, Basil. The hotel's just around the corner from there, and we'll be starting out from a little bit of America."

"Except that Texas isn't exactly a *little* bit of the United States."

"Well, hush mah mouth."

"Hey, Kate," Apple said admiringly, "you do the accent extremely well."

"Thanks. How about you? Are you slow on the drawl?"

"I'm not in your class."

"I'm sure you'll be fine," Kate said. "Now. What shall we do for additional stage dressing?"

"One suitcase will do. I'll attend to that."

"Right. And the next thing is, I want to know about last night."

Apple began with the Caveman Club and how he had cleverly managed to get in. He left out of his story only the sexual aspect, for personal reasons, and the interview with Angus Watkin, on account of need-to-know. He put in a fast exit from the glamorous prostitute's room, during which, on the dark stairs, he had cut his eyebrow.

Kate said, "But your honour was undamaged."

"Very much so."

After they had talked over what Anne had had to say about Alexander Grishin, Apple related the evening's final scene. He confessed, "I have no idea what it means or who this man is."

"Have you seen him before?"

"I'm not sure about that either. And it's just occurred to me, he could've been a common burglar. He'd just gained an entry or had already burgled one of the other flats and hit me to make his escape."

"I suppose that's possible," Kate said. She sounded

nearly as disappointed as Apple felt himself. He wished he hadn't had the idea.

While listening to comments on his action-packed night, Apple wondered if he should describe Beaver to Kate; that might trigger a recollection in her mind. It might also make her think him a jump-at-shadows amateur.

Kate asked, "And your lady of the oldest profession was a really glamorous creature, mm?"

Hoping it wasn't a Porter-hear that told him Kate's voice held an edge of jealousy, Apple redescribed Anne in less flattering terms. Being poor at invention, he gave her the thin body of soprano Maude, the haughty manner of Carolina Winterdale-Moore, and the boxerish face of Patsy. He added Jock Ward's lisp. He would have gone on but felt that he might start to overdo it.

After a hastened good-bye, Apple disconnected and left the telephone kiosk. He began to wend his way north. His gait had less trudge and his head was higher: time, the only known cure, had been steadily at work on his hangover.

At home, not taking off his trench coat, Apple questioned which to do first, have lunch or bring his report up to date. Furthermore, in respect of the latter, did Beaver go into it or not? If yes, and if Angus Watkin demanded to see the report before the mission was over, he could conclude that Beaver was a Hammer, meaning that Apple had been rumbled and therefore should be pulled out.

The telephone rang.

Turning down his coat collar as a concession to being indoors, Apple crossed to the corner table and lifted the receiver. Before he could speak, the voice of Ogden Renfrew said with stagey huffiness:

"I've been trying to get you for the past two hours, you damned elusive Pimpernel."

"Sorry about that, Og."

"Never mind, I've got you now," the actor said. "I've got you and I've got news."

"Of Ethel?"

"Yes, lad, yes. She's found. Come at once."

Apple burst out of his flat, thundered down the stairs, careened around the hallway's centre table and fumbled his way out to the street. There, he made himself stride briskly instead of run.

He thought: Calm, Porter. Steady head. Cool's the word. Ethel won't run away. And if you gallop like a maniac, you might fall and break a limb.

His mind settling to clarity, Apple decided that he would do now what he was going to do later: rent a car. It would take longer than getting a cab—if one could be found now in the noon rush—but, because he could speed, the actual driving time would be shorter between here and Putney.

On the telephone Apple hadn't waited for details on how, only asking for the where. Ogden Renfrew had said, "Let us meet outside the White Swan, a pub in Putney High Street. Tarry not, lad."

But Apple thought it sensible to tarry, at least for as long as it took him to settle matters in the car-hire office, where said matters would be expedited by the fact of his being an old customer.

Apple was soon on Theobald's Road. He marched into the office and came to a snapped, military halt at the counter. The girl behind it winced. She had large spectacles that magnified her mien of apprehension.

Slapping down his credit card, Apple explained that he was in a hurry. "So if you'd be kind enough to fill in the form for me, Miss Smith, I'll go straight through to the garage."

"By all means, Mr. Porter."

Apple grabbed a form and signed on the dotted line. "Grey or black, please."

The girl, who had been heading for a block of pigeon-holes, stopped and turned. "Are you serious, Mr. Porter?"

"Certainly. Of course. I'll settle for dark brown."

Blinking worriedly: "But you always take bright colours. You insist on them. You're a one for your reds and lime greens and yellows."

"Not today," Apple said. "Something quiet, please."

"There's a lovely chartreuse with a white top that I've had my eye on for you, Mr. Porter. Except that you haven't been in lately."

"No, Miss Smith. Dark colour only."

The enlarged eyes closed and opened slowly, coolly. "Very well, sir. I only work here, of course."

Two minutes later Apple was driving a dark grey Honda. Again he had to admonish himself to take it easy. The situation wouldn't be helped if he had an accident.

Even so, Apple drove with a good deal less than caution as he zipped in and out of traffic, heading west and south. He told his reproving self that this was good practice for what was to come later.

To help in staying medium calm, Apple kept his mind off Ethel, as he had managed to do with fair success ever since her disappearance.

At last Apple reached Putney and drove along the suburb's main business street. He picked out ahead the sign of the White Swan pub.

Under the sign, as he drew closer, Apple saw that not only was Ogden Renfrew waiting there but also everyone else from the search party.

Noticing him in the car when he flashed his lights, the group responded with grinding animation. The ex-policeman saluted. Maude waved a handkerchief furiously. The gross Jim Hall jumped up in the air. Alf, landlord of the Bellringer Arms, gestured an invitation towards the pub's entrance. Patsy lifted clasped hands in a champ's salute.

As Apple drew abreast and stopped, Duke Ellington strode to the car and pulled the door open. The others crowded up behind, everyone talked at once, the three women got into the back, Apple turned his smile from face to face while piecing the story together.

Jock Ward, the sometime auctioneer, who was from this area, had found Ethel. Snooping alleys, he had passed behind a small paint-and-body shop. In the cindered yard stood the ex-taxi, glistening with new black paint.

Shrewdly leaving the situation as was, Jock had tried calling the Bloomsbury flat, had failed to make contact, had called all the others to spread the good word.

"We decided to come in force," John Blake said. "In case of trouble with the miscreants."

Carolina Winterdale-Moore showed her fist. "If they get violent . . ."

"We can't go wrong, being team-handed," Alf said.

Maude, pointing, said thinly, "You've already had some trouble, Apple, it appears."

"No, I fell out of bed. I was having a nightmare about losing my holidays."

"We're wasting time," Jim Hall said. "You follow us."

He and the other men turned briskly away and went along the street. They formed an odd-looking band. The women on the back seat murmured admiringly, and Patsy said that she fancied that there Duke something rotten.

Apple drove on. He followed around a corner and along a street and parked in the place which each of the men indicated with important gestures. He and the women got out. "Shh," everyone told him as the group went into a service lane.

They stopped by a wide gateway. Beyond was the yard, with no signs of life around the building it backed, though from inside came bodywork noises. There were three vehicles, all newly painted. Smiling richly at the black one, Apple hurried forwards for the formality of a positive identification.

Once upon a time, at the frozen summit of the Cold War, a group of NATO espionage operatives with nothing better to do had made a bet as to who could locate the celebrated Ethel first. A Canadian won, in two and a half hours, and as proof scratched his initials near the radiator. It was some time later that a Hammer, in derision, had added underneath the letters USSR.

Apple bent down at the front of the taxi. He searched with his eyes and then with his fingers. The engraved graffiti was not there. The vehicle was not Ethel.

Apple drooped, inside and out. After straightening the outside slowly, he turned. Standing nearby, in a crescent, were his friends. Each was looking at him with a shy, quiet smile, one of pleasure for self and in appreciation of the pleasure being experienced by Apple.

He sighed. Spreading his hands, he said, "Thank you for finding Ethel for me."

Apple had lost his disappointment by the time he awoke from a siesta that afternoon. For one thing, there was still hope through paying ransom. For another, his subconscious, as though to answer that lie about a nightmare, had come up with a dream wherein he and Ethel were bowling merrily along a golden highway. All, he felt positive, would come out right in the end.

Noisily yawning, Apple headed for the bathroom to treat himself to a long, hot soak.

Behind the body shop, Apple had got his friends away by explaining that he would do nothing about Ethel at the moment; as a form of revenge, he would let his

Institute colleagues think they had won, not telling them
he had found Ethel until the very last minute. All but
Carolina Winterdale-Moore approved of the strategy.

To strengthen his pretense as well as offer a thank-you
for assistance, Apple had hosted the group at a celebra-
tion lunch in the White Swan. It was a boisterous affair.
The wine got to everyone except Apple, who thought it
best not to indulge. He smiled bravely through John
Blake's anecdotes of arrests he had nearly made,
Maude's slim singing, Duke Ellington's piano playing,
Jim Hall's clog dance and Ogden Renfrew's moving ren-
dition of "Albert and the Lion." It was almost four
o'clock before Apple was able to get away.

Dry from his bath, underclothes donned, Apple went
in the spare room and chose a suitcase from among his
collection. He filled it with yellowed newspapers and
some old bones of Monico's.

In his bedroom Apple began to dress—after first tap-
ing the envelope of money onto his chest. He put on a
check shirt that he usually wore only for the cottage,
jeans and denim jacket. Boots on, he stuffed the jeans
into their tops. A string tie he fashioned out of the blue
ribbon that had been around a Christmas present.

Wobbling on his high heels, Apple went to the flat
door. He put on his ten-gallon hat and looked in the
mirror. He was pleased. He thought that he could un-
doubtedly pass for a tough, scarred cowpuncher on a
European vacation.

Apple tried a drawl. It sounded terrible. He jerked
away from the mirror with a false laugh and left the flat.
His laugh he held in readiness at the back of his throat in
case he met anyone on the way down.

Outdoors, about to follow his suitcase into the Honda,
Apple remembered the Stetson. He took it off and tossed
it onto the case, got in, drove off.

Apple had time to spare, as planned, and on reaching

Grosvenor Square he saw that he had been right to think well ahead. Every parking slot was taken, with cars idling around to grab what came available. Apple joined the idlers, both on the square and in off-streets.

Twenty minutes passed before he got lucky. He parked, got out, put on his hat, took it off again and carried it and the suitcase over to the centre of the square, to the Roosevelt Memorial.

Apple recalled that just after World War II the British people were asked to contribute to the fifty thousand pounds needed for the creation of a memorial to the late American President, with no donation to exceed five shillings and that the target was reached in twenty-three hours and twenty-two minutes.

Soon, Kate appeared. Her outfit was the same as Apple's except that she wore a skirt instead of jeans. Also, like Apple, she was carrying her Stetson. As they walked to a meeting, they both donned their hats. They laughed with each other for not laughing at each other.

Following a minute of talk, they went over to the side of the square. Apple was managing better now on his high heels, but was far from feeling secure.

As he and Kate walked to the nearby hotel, they stopped more than one person dead in his tracks. They got more of the same in the hotel lobby, which was large and old-fashioned, with potted palms spaced around among the leather furniture.

At an ornate reception desk, a middle-aged man with white curls stared upwards nervously. He said, "May I be of assistance?"

Using her drawl, Kate asked if there were vacancies. As expected, March being off-season, the clerk said there were.

"That's real nice," Kate said. "We'd like to have room 315, please. Wouldn't we, Hank?"

Apple said, "Mmm." Glancing around, he saw that they had an avid audience.

The man craned upwards again after checking in a ledger. His nervousness had become relief. "Sorry," he said, "but 315 is taken."

Kate put on an expression of anguish. "Oh my. That's terrible. We just got to have that little old room. It's where Hank and me spent our honeymoon, five years ago this week. Didn't we, Hank?"

"Mmm."

Changing his manner again, now to a show of interest, the clerk brought from under the counter a different ledger. "Five years ago, ma'am?"

"That's right."

"What is the name, please?"

Kate leaned down on her elbows. "We don't remember."

Outdrawling: "Oh."

"See, Hank and me we're kinda old-fangled. We never fooled around before we got married. Know what I mean? No anticipating of them sacred vows and like that. Kinda silly, I guess."

"Not at all," the clerk said with restrained vigour, straightening his back. "Most commendable." He gazed up at them fondly, like a teacher at star pupils.

"So what we did was," Kate went on, "was register under a phony name so's we'd feel naughty, illicit like. I guess that's silly as well."

Indulgently: "We all have our harmless little foibles."

"And the thing is, is we don't remember what name it was we used."

The clerk put the old ledger away and went back over the current one. "How sad that 315 is occupied," he said. "And so is 314."

"Ah," Apple said as a reminder to Kate.

She asked, "Who's in 314 now? Would it, by a wild coincidence, be good old Sam Haines?"

After innocently supplying the information that Alexander Grishin had reserved the room for tonight under the name of Wilson Carver, the clerk said, brightening:

"I see, however, that 313 is vacant."

Smiling, Apple allowed himself a "Good."

But Kate insisted, "It has to be 315. That room means so much to us, y'hear? I don't know what we'll do if we can't get it."

Apple nudged her, but she seemed to be sunk deep in her role, going on to say how brokenhearted she would be and all if they were denied the honeymoon scene.

Apple asked the clerk, "Rooms all the same?"

"More than that, sir. They're identical to the last detail. There's no favouritism at the Brand."

"See?" Apple told Kate loudly and meaningfully.

She said, "I'm going to cry myself to sleep tonight, I just know it, if'n I don't get dear old 315."

The clerk raised a hand. He looked down at the ledger, then up again. His expression now quietly ruthless, he said, "I believe I might be able to persuade the lady in 315 to move to another room."

Kate clapped her hands. "Why, that's just wonderful."

"I'm sure you won't mind waiting. It will only take an hour or so."

"313 will do," Apple said firmly, flatly. He gave Kate a strong nudge. "Right, honey?"

She blinked. "What? Oh yes. Sure."

The clerk shook his head emphatically. "No. Sentiment must be served. There's little enough of it in this day and age. I will personally interview the lady in 315."

Apple swung the ledger around, picked up a pen and signed. Next to Hank West, under room numbers, he put "313" in a heavy hand.

Changing to wistfulness, the clerk said, "Please. One hour. I guarantee success."

Apple slapped out his hand palm up. "The key, please. And thank you for your help."

By modern hotel standards, the room was of ample proportions. Opening out from the short passage between the bathroom and the storage area for clothes and luggage, it was about twenty feet square.

A lithograph above the twin beds of the hotel's Scottish counterpart faced a litho of its colleague in Wales, which hung over the dressing table. Both were screwed into place. The wallpaper was a melange of flowers and figures.

Apple, who had declined staff help with the suitcase, put it away and went to draw the curtains. When that was done he said, "Mr. Wilson Carver hasn't arrived yet. The key was in its pigeonhole."

"So I saw," Kate said, appearing from the bathroom. She carried an empty glass. "I hope this is going to work."

"It usually does, but a lot depends on the thickness of the walls."

Taking her hat off, Kate went to the wall behind the beds. With an ear to the glass's base and its mouth flat on the wallpaper, she listened.

"Yes," she said. "The line's fuzzy but I can hear a radio playing. I can make out the lyrics."

"Great."

"But maybe that's because I know the song. You try."

Apple removed his Stetson and took over at the wall. He could hear music but no words. "It's not so good," he said, turning away. "Better than nothing, however."

"Let's hope that our Alex and his friend speak nice and clearly when they arrive."

Apple was looking around the room. "Identical," he said thoughtfully.

"What's that, Basil?"

"Alex's room. It's exactly the same as this. Same paper, same pictures. So it might work."

"What might?"

Smiling, eager, Apple said, "We make a hole through the wall. Right under the Welsh litho. It should come out immediately under the Scottish picture next door."

"Yes, I see," Kate said slowly. "I think you've got something there."

"And look at our Scots deal. It has a good inch of shadow under the bottom of the frame from the ceiling light. That would help obscure the hole, as well as the wallpaper being of the busy type."

Kate joined his eagerness. "But we needn't break right through the paper. All we'd need for better hearing is to get close to it."

"Of course. So do we have a go?"

"Yes, we do."

"Okay," Apple said. "You measure the height of the frame from the floor while I see if I can find something to use as a tool."

"Try the bathroom."

There was nothing there, nor in the storage area, nor on the vanity table. As a last hope he looked in the two drawers of the tween-beds table and found only that the Gideons had been, the Gideons had been.

Kate meanwhile, using a coat hanger and fingernail scratches, had discovered that both pictures were hung at the same height.

"Hopefully, it'll be the same next door."

"Perfect," Apple said. "All we need now is an implement of some kind."

"Maybe that lovely man at the desk can help."

Apple was grateful for the cue. He had been on the

point of saying that he would get a screwdriver from his rented car. But he didn't particularly want Kate to know about the car or what he had to do later.

"Of course he'll help," he said, grabbing his ten-gallon hat. "Be right back."

Hurrying down the stairs, which seemed faster than using a lift, Apple put his Stetson on at a forwards, face-hiding tilt, in case Alexander Grishin came early and saw him and found him familiar. In any event, Apple hoped to pass through the lobby unobtrusively.

He had no intentions of going to the desk. A hotel guest asking to borrow a tool could only arouse suspicion at least, and at most the insistence that staff take care of whatever job it was that needed doing.

Apple came into the lobby. He set off across it at a sagging lope. He looked about as unobtrusive as a pipe in a nun's mouth. It was no help that at one stage, circling a potted palm, he wobbled dangerously on his high heels.

Except for the wobble, Apple's return crossing was a repeat, after he had taken a screwdriver from the Honda's tool kit. Again also there was no sign of the Russian.

Back in 313 Apple flung his hat aside and brought the tool from out of his sleeve. He set to work directly under the frame of the Welsh hotel lithograph, twisting the screwdriver rapidly in a half circle and biting into the plaster.

There was plenty of time, Apple assured himself. He had over half an hour before he needed to leave for his rendezvous in Primrose Hill.

Soon, minor debris was falling from the hole onto the dressing table. Kate began removing handfuls at regular intervals to flush down the lavatory.

Apple paused—to give his working arm a rest, to check his watch, to gauge how far the hole had progressed. About half an inch, he reported.

"And I imagine these partition walls are between two and three inches thick."

"We ought to do it in time then."

There was a knock on the door.

Apple and Kate looked at each other. Apple whispered, "Maybe it's Alex. Maybe he's been in there all along. Maybe he's come to complain."

Kate whispered, "What can we do?"

"Answer from inside. We don't open the door unless we have to."

"I'll do it. He's seen less of me than he has of you."

Apple wiped debris off the table and moved to a sit on a bed. He heard Kate, along the short passage, ask who it was and a boy's voice answer, "Compliments of the hotel for Mr. and Mrs. West." The door opened. It closed again after Kate had said a warm "Thank you very much." She reappeared with a bunch of flowers in a vase.

"Isn't that sweet? And there's a card. It wishes us a happy second honeymoon."

Apple looked at his watch. There was twenty minutes to go until departure time. He returned to his work with fresh determination, grinding away in the hole.

After a moment, Apple glanced around to see why Kate had become remiss in her job as debris remover. He saw that she was moving back from having changed again the position of the vase of flowers on the tween-table.

Kate, Apple thought, was acting a little oddly this evening, though he reminded himself that it could be his own growing nervousness that was making him see it that way.

He worked on.

Kate started to do her job. She asked to be let have a turn at grinding. Her turn was brief: unthinkingly, Apple had set the hole at the level of his own ear, a height which Kate found awkward.

Apple went back to drilling. His shoulder and wrist ached, his palm was sore from gripping the screwdriver, his stomach throbbed with tension.

"Not much time left," Kate said.

Grinding viciously, Apple gasped, "No." But he was thinking less of Alexander Grishin's arrival next door than of the date at Primrose Hill.

The minutes passed. There was no sound in the room other than the grind of metal on brick, Apple's heavy breathing and the squeak as Kate wiped debris from the table's glass top. Apple longed for a break and a cigarette, but he had to keep on working.

He gave an extra-heavy, twisting push—and he was abruptly through to the other side, the screwdriver blade slamming in the hole up to its handle.

Sagging hugely (Kate stroking his back in congratulation), Apple rested a moment before withdrawing his tool. He closed one eye and peered in the half-inch-diameter hole.

Although there was no light on in the next room, its curtains were drawn back, allowing the penetration of street lighting. Most of the room was visible.

Apple turned. "This is far better than I expected," he said. "Not only will we be able to hear, we'll be able to see as well. Have a look."

While Kate was getting herself into a kneel on the dressing table, Apple checked his watch. He was alarmed to see that it showed ten minutes to eight. At eight he was due to meet the carnappers.

"Fabulous," Kate said, peering. "And any debris that's fallen on the other side'll be hidden, down behind the table between the beds."

"I have to go," Apple said.

Kate looked around. "What?"

"I—um—have to take the screwdriver back to the clerk."

"Now?"

"At once. Immediately. Right away."

Kate said, "But Alex'll be showing up at any minute."

Apple put his hat on. "Exactly. And everything could be ruined if the clerk comes pounding on the door, looking for his screwdriver."

"But, Basil . . ."

"No problem," Apple said, backing towards the passage. "No problem whatever. You'll be here to listen." He turned away. "See you soon."

Striding implacably across the hotel lobby, Apple thought that he could worry later about creating a story to cover his absence, which, if all went well, would only be some twenty minutes.

Outside, however, breaking into a run, Apple mused that the story would have to be particularly good. He had just realised that, in his haste to leave, he had left the screwdriver behind.

Apple reached the Honda. With a groan, he saw that it had been all but blocked in. It stood bumper to bumper with the vehicle in front, a short foot away from the car behind.

After a second or two of remaining stock still, Apple swung back into fast action. He got inside after his black Stetson, started the motor, slapped the gearstick into first and eased the Honda forwards carefully but strongly, riding his clutch.

The car ahead was pushed forwards several inches. Apple held there until he had fought the steering wheel around, then slammed in the clutch but didn't need to change to reverse: the built-up pressure was enough to shoot the Honda backwards. Again he started wrestling the wheel.

Two more similar shunts, and Apple had the space to get clear. He cut out and shot away.

Although rush hour had passed, there was still ample traffic in this central area, much of it carrying sightseers at a dawdle. Apple whipped around cars at jerked speed. He blasted his horn, flashed his lights, shouted unheard at road-hoggers.

Not until he was on the straight stretch of Gloucester Place was he able to get his foot to the floor with some hopes of keeping it there for more than a few seconds. But he continued to violate every unwritten and official rule of the Queen's highway.

What helped Apple to resist looking at his watch was the danger of splitting his attention. In any case, he assured himself, if he were a little late, it wouldn't matter. The carnappers, who were in this racket for profit, would surely make return trips.

In circling Regent's Park, Apple was able to hit higher speeds. He went through deserted traffic lights on red, passed a bus on the inside lane and went into a wide, tyre-screeching arc to round the final corner.

Apple parked where he'd had the taxi wait the last time he was here. Quickly he delved inside his check shirt, freed the envelope of money from its tapes, brought it out.

Alighting, Apple took his hat with him on an afterthought, which proved sound a moment later, when he arrived at the position by Primrose Hill's rails: with his Stetson on he felt stronger.

Now he looked at his watch. The time was two minutes past eight o'clock. Apple didn't know whether to fret over being late or to preen over having done the journey in record time.

A car was coming. Apple's nerves twitched when the headlights dipped. But they didn't come up again and the routine called for several dippings. This driver was merely being polite, so as not to bedazzle the pedestrian.

The next car kept its lights up, as did the following half

dozen. Also they all reduced speed acutely, going by with the people inside gaping at Apple as though he were about to ask to be taken to their leader.

He began to pace. That he gave up after almost losing his balance on the high heels, which were unsuited to the rough surface underfoot. He stood on the kerb, his envelope prominently on display.

To prevent himself from believing that the carnappers had already been and wouldn't be coming back, Apple forced his mind to the task of creating a cover story for Kate. He had found one by the time three more carloads of rubberneckers had gone by.

He stopped at the reception desk, realised he had left the screwdriver behind and started back. He saw a familiar face. It belonged to a Hammer, one he had seen before, on a caper in Rome. The Hammer was watching him. So, acting a no-tumble, he left the hotel to draw . . .

An approaching car dipped its lights. After a pause, they came up again. Another pause and down they went.

By now the car, moving at about twenty miles an hour, was close enough for Apple to make out details. It was a recent-model Peugeot. There were two people inside, both in the front and both male. Their faces were pale and oddly shaped. It took a longer, harder stare before Apple realised that the men were wearing cheap toyshop masks.

The car was nearly level. Its nearside rear window was rolled down. Apple poised himself and readied the envelope. The car came abreast but well away from the kerb. Apple made his toss. The envelope sailed across and went through the open window.

The Peugeot spurted on.

Apple shouted, "When do I get my car back?"

He hadn't really expected an answer, but the Peugeot began to slow. It came to a stop some twenty or thirty yards on. The passenger reached behind him and got the envelope.

Apple started to walk forwards, hesitantly at first, then with more purpose. He had almost reached the car—its passenger was bent down as if examining the envelope's contents—when it moved on and shot ahead.

Apple slowed to a stop. He was surprised to see that the Peugeot did precisely the same, again at a distance of around twenty-five yards.

Noting now that he was in a steady beam of light from behind, Apple glanced back. He had an audience. Two cars were coming along at a crawl, their passengers leaning forwards to stare.

Apple turned back to face the Peugeot. Cupping both hands to his mouth he called, "These people aren't with me!"

There being no word or sign from the carnappers, he moved towards them at a faster stride. At once, the Peugeot repeated its former performance, completely, going on but coming to a stop when Apple halted.

They were playing a game with him, Apple thought, raging quietly. Or they didn't want to leave the scene until they'd counted the money. Or this teasing was for some reason that he couldn't fathom.

Apple tensed. Quickly he reflected that if he made an abrupt, full-out dash forwards, he might be able to get to the car before the driver had it moving. He could pull him out, hold him, make a citizen's arrest. He would get Ethel back, the money back, and break up these particular practitioners of a dirty racket.

Apple was tempted. The people in the cars behind would lend a hand if he couldn't manage the two men himself. But then Apple remembered the cowboy boots. In high heels he wasn't about to do any brilliant sprinting.

Apple decided to leave matters as they stood. Swinging away, he hurried off towards the Honda.

The return trip was satisfyingly fast and uneventful. It was only when he reached the Grosvenor Square area that Apple came up against a problem. There were no parking slots and doubling would have been too obstructive.

The only space Apple saw was the one in front of the Brand Hotel, reserved for the come and go of taxis. Second time around the block, he shot into it, stopping with one wheel up on the kerb.

Leaving his hat, Apple slammed out of the Honda and almost bumped into a burly, uniformed doorman, who blustered, "Can't park here. Not for one second."

"Emergency at the U.S. Embassy," Apple snapped. "Y'all."

"What?"

"But stay calm whatever happens." He pushed past the man and went on in.

Apple quickly crossed the lobby, circling to stay far from the reception desk, where, however, he saw nothing of Alexander Grishin. Using only the soles of his boots, he ran up the stairs.

On the door of 313 Apple tapped out in Morse a fast *BASIL*. After a pause, the door opened—an inch at first and then fully. Kate put a finger to her lips.

She whispered, "Alex came in a few minutes ago."

"Is he alone?"

"So far, yes. Where on earth have you been?" Before Apple could begin on his story, she added, "Never mind now. Come in."

Following inside, Apple whispered, "He hasn't noticed the hole, obviously."

With a forefinger Kate signalled a negative and for complete silence and for Apple to try the peephole. He did. Alexander Grishin was in plain view, sitting on the end of one of the beds, faced the other way. His arms were folded. He looked the epitome of patience.

Apple went on watching through the peephole and Grishin went on sitting. Two minutes passed. Apple's eye began to feel cold. He gestured for Kate to take a turn.

Going to the bed on the right, Apple half sat, half lay, sprawling back on the pillow. He was only just beginning to wind down from his experience with the carnappers, but had started winding up with concern over the consequences of his Honda's position.

Would someone knock on the door or telephone? Either sound would be sure to be heard in the next room.

Apple took the receiver off its cradle. He had just settled back again when Kate suddenly turned. She took two quick steps forwards, which brought her into the space between the beds.

Apple looked questioningly at Kate's face. It was without expression. Next, Apple became alarmed as his twin started to raise her arms, doing so slowly and sinuously like a belly dancer about to perform.

Apple stared.

After waving her hands on high, Kate brought them down in a floating movement and began to take off her denim jacket. At the same time, as if taking over from the arms, her hips swayed rhythmically from side to side.

Apple stared, now in astonishment. He considered the possibility that Kate was temporarily out of her mind. She had, after all, acted oddly already this evening.

Apple noted that Kate was looking at him fixedly while moving her lips. She made no sound. He wondered about that until his attention was drawn away by the jacket falling to the floor.

Swaying seductively, Kate pulled undone her string tie and started unfastening buttons. With the last one free, she drew up her shirt out of the jeans and slipped it first off one shoulder and next off the other. She was nude underneath.

Apple tried to look back at the lips, which, he sensed, were still moving, but he found that he was mesmerised by the naked breasts and the hands that were now undoing the belt buckle.

When her jeans were open at the top, displaying a V of white panties, Kate raised one leg forwards while lifting her arms for balance. The message was quite clear: *Remove my boot, please.*

Dazedly, Apple leaned up, grasped the fancy footwear and drew it off. When Kate changed legs he did the same with the other boot. He eased back into his sprawl and looked up at the quietly animated face.

Kate, of course, was mouthing words, Apple realised, so what he had to do was concentrate in order to lip-read. But again his attention was drawn irresistibly away by her hands which were back at work.

The jeans descended slowly, to thighs and then knees, revealing fully the white briefs that were the briefest Apple had ever seen. He clenched his toes.

Kate stepped out of her jeans. After turning herself in a languid circle, she used delicately pincered finger and thumb at either side to pluck outward the top of her panties. She began to draw the garment down, the while bringing her trunk forwards and down, so that when the white material had been taken below the protected area, that area was immediately hidden by Kate's head.

Apple's chest felt tight. A lot of him felt tight. He clenched and relaxed his toes spasmodically.

Briefs removed, Kate slowly brought her trunk erect. She put both hands to the nape of her neck and posed exotically. She was statuesque and magnificent.

Apple's glance roved nervously and greedily to take in all the salient points. He gave eye caresses to thigh and hip, flat stomach and thrusting breast. He even looked once at Kate's mouth. It had become motionless, he was distantly relieved to note.

Kate ended her pose. She came to the bed and slowly lowered herself onto it beside Apple. Covering him with an arm and a leg, she snuggled her face in beside his. Her mouth was on his ear.

In a tone so low that it was barely audible, she murmured, "Alex discovered the peephole."

Apple flicked his eyes over the far wall. Without looking directly at the hole, he saw that, whereas earlier it had been a spot of brightness from the light beyond, now it was dark; blocked, he understood, by the watcher's face.

Kate whispered, "It's time to act a split, right?"

Apple nodded.

Kate sat up. "Oh well," she said in a normal voice," if you're not in the mood, hon, we might as well go catch that movie. Okay by you?"

"Sure."

Kate got off the bed and began to dress. Since Apple himself had no preparation to do, it was only natural that he should watch the striptease in reverse, he thought. He also thought that as Alexander Grishin had already had a good view of his face, there was no point in trying to hide it. He watched the show gladly, though with a wistfulness for what might have been.

Keeping up a flow of natural-sounding comment on this swell movie they'd heard about, Kate got her clothes on. Apple joined her at the passage. He opened the door, switched off the light, closed the door again noisily.

Ten minutes had passed. There was silence in both rooms. Apple and Kate stood one on either side of the peephole, through which Apple took occasional, fleeting glances, and from which there came enough light for him to make out his immediate surroundings.

Use of the peephole was denied Kate, who might create a noise if she tried climbing up on the dressing table or using some other type of elevation. As it was, she and Apple were keeping as still as possible. They hadn't spoken since their pretend exit, but had communicated by means of signals or finger-pressure Morse.

Apple had used mime to congratulate Kate on her presence of mind when she had seen Alexander Grishin approaching the peephole. Cleverly, allayingly, she had turned him from the spied-on into a voyeur. Kate had responded to Apple's congratulations by sinking into a curtsy, forefinger cutely under chin.

Grishin was back sitting on the bed, arms folded, waiting without a sign of impatience.

The silence was shattered by a knocking.

Apple's body jerked. That had to be someone about the car, he thought. There was no need, however, to answer. But what if it was a maid? If she got no reply, she'd come in and that would be the end of it.

Apple had a flash of anger at himself for not having had the sense to hang out a do-not-disturb card.

Quickly he looked in the peephole. Alexander Grishin had gone from sight.

Only then did Apple realise that the knock had been at the door of the other room.

There came the sound of a latch clicking. Apple next heard a voice say "You're late." As it patently came from this side of the door, Apple accepted the voice as belonging to Alexander Grishin.

"I got delayed," another male voice said. "There was a traffic holdup."

"Something deliberate?"

"No, nothing like that."

"Come in."

Grishin reappeared. He went to the bed and took up his former position, even to the extent of folding his arms. He said, again speaking English, "These innocent-seeming delays can, of course, be easily arranged, as we know. But in this case it is improbable simply because it would be pointless."

The accent was excellent, Apple expertly allowed with some surprise. He himself would need to listen with care to detect that the English wasn't native to the speaker—after first having had his suspicions aroused by the very excellence of the accent when coupled with a pedantic speech manner.

"In any case," Alexander Grishin said, "I was a number of minutes late myself, so I can hardly complain."

"Quite," the other man said. He had not come into view, except as a slice of dark blue suiting at the edge of the peephole's range. He seemed to be leaning on a corner of the passage.

Grishin asked, "Would you care to sit?"

"I'm fine," the man said. "Anyway, this isn't exactly a social call."

A crawling sensation went down Apple's spine. There was something familiar about the voice of the stranger, who was definitely British.

"True," the Russian said. "On the other hand, we need not act like characters in an underworld drama."

The unseen man gave a short laugh, and again Apple got the crawling sensation. He was positive now that he knew the voice's owner, but was unable to do any relating. A glance aside at Kate showed him that she hadn't had a similar response of recognition.

"To the point, however," Alexander Grishin said. "You work for British Intelligence, you stated in your note."

"Correct."

"How do I know you're not a doubler? Isn't that what they're called, doublers?"

"It is, and you don't know."

"Rather awkward, that."

The stranger said, "I could even be one of your own people, checking you out."

"That is hardly likely."

"Neither is it likely that I'd be a doubler."

"Why not?"

"Because I'm not important enough. There's nothing I could give Moscow that'd be worth a damn. Not yet."

Alexander Grishin nodded slowly. "But in time?"

The unseen man said, "Two, three, five years from now, certainly. When they elevate me from my placid little posting in North Sea Oil."

Apple nearly had it then. It was as if a face had flashed in and out of his mind, like a subliminal spark. It left nothing behind.

"All this is out of my field, of course," Alexander Grishin said. "Perhaps you would care to tell me why you want to do this thing."

The stranger stated, "Money."

"Ah, yes."

"I want to be put on a monthly retainer, starting as soon as possible. It might pay off for the Russians sometime, or it might not. I have no idea. But those're my terms."

"No ideology involved?"

"None at all. Communism interests me no more than does democracy. They're both failures."

Grishin asked, "Bitterness?"

"That, yes. Over finance. A friend of mine got killed and I got badly mangled. His widow receives a pittance pension, I get next to nothing."

"When was the accident?"

"In Naples last autumn."

"When two CIA agents were also killed? A car bomb?"

"Right," the stranger said. "I didn't think you'd know about that."

"One hears about these things. The diplomatic world is very gossipy. Childishly so."

Following a pause, into the peephole's range came a hand. It held a packet. The stranger asked, "Smoke?"

Alexander Grishin said, "I prefer my own, thank you." As the hand retreated, he brought from a side pocket a flat cardboard box. The cigarette he took from it was brown with a black tip.

Casually, speaking Russian, Grishin asked, "Do you have a light?"

The other man said, "What was that?"

In English: "Sorry. This brand always sends me home in mind. Have you got a match, please?"

The stranger came into full view. His face was obscured by a hat and by the fact that he was half turned away while fishing in a pocket. But his body was plump. Apple, with a catch of his breath, had the answer before the man straightened to show the scar on his cheek. He was Bill Burton.

The following minutes of the interview were lost to Apple, though he sensed that more of the same cat-and-mousing was going on. He worked furiously at trying to understand, or excuse, or refute. Several times, at speed, he flicked back over the foregoing dialogue.

At last, with a surge of relief, Apple found the solution to the matter of loyalty by recalling Bill Burton's reference to North Sea Oil.

Having seen the scar-faced agent at fairly regular intervals, Apple felt that it was unlikely that Burton was in that field of operations. Which reminded Apple that Bill couldn't have been in Naples last autumn either: they had worked together then on a caper.

So, Apple thought, this had to be one of Angus

Watkin's convolutions, and the solution to *that* was anybody's guess, the wilder the better.

The men in the other room had put out their cigarettes. Bill Burton was now sitting on the other bed and the ambiance was less prickly, if not exactly warm.

"What it comes down to," Alexander Grishin said, "is that you want me to act as middleman between you and my country's espionage people."

"I had to start somewhere."

"You realise, of course, that international law prohibits those in diplomatic service from involving themselves in spying activities."

Bill Burton said dryly, "I know a few good jokes myself."

"I don't think they will be necessary."

"But look. You don't have to play middleman for long. Just give me a direction or an introduction."

Thoughtfully, Alexander Grishin said, "That is, I suppose, possible."

"It's the least you can do."

"Perhaps."

"But if you think I'm wasting my time, please say so. I'll forget the whole thing."

"Possibly I should ask for advice first."

Bill Burton shrugged. "I have no idea. But I'm in a hurry. If there's no interest here, then I'll go somewhere else. Probably the Chinese."

"Well now," Grishin said. "I do not see the need for hasty decisions."

"If I don't push, this thing could drag on for months."

"Hardly that."

"It's unimportant to me who I work for. Fortunately, there's more than one outlet for my goods."

"When you have some to sell."

Bill Burton shrugged again. He got up with a show of impatience. "We don't seem to be getting anywhere."

Alexander Grishin also rose. He said, "There is, it has just occurred to me, someone to whom I could introduce you."

"When?"

"Now, as a matter of fact. I could take you to see him in my car. It's parked nearby. Then I can wash my hands of the whole business."

"Fine. That suits me. It's the top men I ought to be talking to in any case."

"All right," Alexander Grishin said. "We shall go at once." He looked around the room with a self-asked "Now, have I got everything?"

Bill Burton went from sight. Grishin's next movements were swift. His back towards the passage, he half pulled from his inside left breast pocket an object that gave off a glint of black metal. He flicked a catch, put the object away again, turned and followed Bill Burton.

The light went out. The door clicked shut.

Apple fumbled his way over to the window and swept the curtains aside. Light from the street came into the room. Going back to Kate, Apple said urgently:

"Alex has a gun. I have the distinct impression that he's not taking Mr. X to see anyone, but is going to kill him."

"Why on earth would he do that?"

"Again, only an impression, a feeling. Alex could be playing his own renegade game, and he thinks this phony traitor is KGB."

Kate blinked. "Phony?"

"Mr. X is one of ours. I know him."

"Christ. And he might get killed."

"If it's as I suspect, yes," Apple said. "And don't forget that Hammer and Sickle in the bird sanctuary."

"True. They might've been doing as heavy an I-spy on Alex as we were."

"It doesn't look good."

Kate asked, "What do we do?"

"Follow, at least," Apple said. "Maybe try to warn Mr. X, without spoiling whatever *his* game is."

"We're in a complicated racket, Basil."

"Let's go."

They hurried out of the room. The corridor was deserted. At a light-footed run they went along to the stairs and started down. Guessing that Alexander Grishin would have used the lift, if only because of the fact that such conveniences had a habit of being out of order in Moscow, Apple brought Kate to a cautious pace at the bottom of the last flight.

Grishin, however, was already at the reception desk, with Bill Burton waiting nearby. The scar-faced agent stood looking idly at a display case of china. He didn't catch the movement when Apple waved, and a moment later joined Grishin in walking towards the exit.

About to move forwards from the foot of the stairs, Apple and Kate were stopped by an advancing body of large people. They wore grins and the colourful dress of tourists. Their leader, a buxom matron, said piercingly, "You folks just have to be from Oklahoma."

"Texas," Apple said, trying to push past among cries of howdy and say there.

The matron, beaming: "The Panhandle, I bet. That's almost as good as being an Okie."

Apple, seeing that Grishin and Bill Burton had left the hotel, kept pushing. He said, "New Orleans."

"That ain't in Texas," one of the men said.

Another, frowning, accused, "And you sure do talk funny."

The matron, her smile slipshod, said, "I guess you could be from that old Fort Worth."

"We're imposters," Kate said. "Excuse, please." Behind Apple, she gave him a hard shove. He burst roughly through the human barrier and went lurching on.

They reached the main door. Even before going through, Apple could see that his Honda was still on the reserved space. He went outside and was faced at once by the doorman, who said smugly, "The police nearly towed it away."

"Good," Apple said absently, switching his head in search of the Russian and Bill Burton. He could see no signs of them.

"It would've cost you a pretty penny to get it back," the doorman said threateningly.

"There!" Kate whispered fiercely, pointing.

Fifty feet away, a black Rover was pulling out into the narrow street from a parking space. Alexander Grishin sat at the wheel. The car's direction was the opposite of that faced by the Honda.

"My car," Kate said.

"And mine," Apple said. "This one. We'll fore-and-aft."

Kate moved off hastily. "Hurry up and turn."

Apple was stopped from moving towards his Honda by the bulky doorman, who said, grim, "I done you a favour." He obviously was determined to get compensation. He wanted his pound of money.

Apple slapped pockets, located cash, dragged some of it out and thrust it into the waiting hand. Reminding himself in a fast-passing thought that he would have to go back to the Brand soonest to pay the bill, Apple snapped, "Stand back."

He strode to the car and got in. Starting the motor, he battled the wheel around and shot briefly forwards, lurching to a stop with the front bumper almost in the hotel entrance. He reversed after another wheel fight and was out in the roadway. He zoomed off.

Kate's Fiesta soon came into view. It was separated

from the Honda by a taxi. Apple left it that way for the time being. The black Rover, he saw on taking a bend, was similarly spaced, two vehicles between itself and the Fiesta.

In this manner, several streets were covered. Since there had been opportunities for Kate to pass the vehicles, as a start to getting beyond the mark's car, Apple concluded that she wanted him to play that part in the fore-and-aft.

When the next clear stretch came, he spurted the Honda forwards, pulled out and passed the taxi. The way was still clear. Speeding on he went by Kate (attempting no signal) and managed to pass one of the vehicles ahead. Oncoming traffic filled in again.

The Rover took several corners and went through two sets of traffic lights, being held at one. Apple found that his palms were sweaty. He wiped them on his jeans.

A minute later, the truck in front of Apple turned off. There was only Alexander Grishin's Rover ahead. Glancing in his rear-view mirror, Apple saw that the intervener behind had also gone. The Fiesta was right there.

The Rover turned at Marble Arch and began to sweep around the island. Because of the angle, Apple had a clear sighting on the occupants of the car ahead. Grishin and Bill Burton were sitting solemn-faced.

Apple looked around. He noted Kate and was about to face front again when something familiar made him stare at the car behind the Fiesta; or rather, at the two people in its front seat.

The car was a large old Daimler. In it sat a couple who bore a strong resemblance to the Hammer and Sickle from the bird sanctuary.

Apple turned away. As he did, he was surprised to see that the Rover was starting on another circle of the island. He also realised that its speed had increased. Lowering his foot to close the gap, he looked around again.

This time, the light being better at this point on the road, Apple was sure. The man and woman in the Daimler were the ones with whom he and Kate had battled. Their expressions hinted at purpose.

After a check on his driving, Apple had another look behind. That his scan went beyond the Daimler was automatic. He expected nothing. But what he saw in yet another car was a man with a full, dark beard.

"Christ," Apple said. "It's a parade."

The Rover turned off. Apple followed. With glances in his rear-view mirror, he checked that also following was Kate, who was tailed by the Hammer and Sickle, behind whom came the knock-out expert, Beaver.

The last two cars had to go, Apple decided, although he had been unable to make any other decision—that is, what to do about Bill Burton. But whatever he did in that direction would be simplified by the absence of the parade's last members.

Apple reasoned that if Kate left, the others, if they couldn't see too far ahead, would naturally follow. But how was he to go about getting the message to her, short of shouting back through the window? Even if she heard clearly, the others might hear as well.

The answer came from the Rover. In slowing to take a corner, its brake lights flashed.

Apple began to dither his foot on and off the brake pedal, tapping out Morse with the rear red lights. Repeatedly he flashed the letter *K*.

Almost as often, Apple glanced in his mirror. It gave him a good if blurred view of Kate's face, though not feature by feature.

He stopped tapping when the road went into a bend, thinking that the effect might be seen by the parade's tailenders. They wouldn't be able to on the straights, he judged, because of all the other lights flashing around from businesses and vehicles.

With the other cars directly behind him again, Apple went back to tapping out *K*. His third glance in the rear-view was rewarded by seeing Kate giving deliberate nods. He changed to sending his message.

That he was giving a pro what amounted to orders didn't bother Apple. The safety of Bill Burton came before rank and protocol.

The message sending was interrupted at regular intervals by Apple having to turn corners, follow the Rover, which, he noted distantly, seemed to be turning back on its tracks.

Apple didn't need to go right through to the final words of his message. With deep nods and a single flash of her direction signal, Kate let him know that she had got the gist. She began to slow the Fiesta.

The Rover took yet another turn. Apple went around it seconds later. He gave as much attention as he could to his mirror. He smiled on seeing in it first Kate go straight on by, next the Daimler, last the car driven by Beaver.

Apple settled to the task ahead, whatever that might involve. About Kate he had no qualms. He felt sure she would be able to handle the situation if it became physical, but knew she had the savvy to keep her distance.

The Rover went along several more streets. That it had been working around into a horseshoe became clear to Apple when he found himself passing through a broad gateway. They had entered Hyde Park.

The road had no kerbs. It lay level with the flat, smooth grass on either side. Standing back were delicate palings, intended more as demarcation than barriers. Here in the park, headlights were the only form of illumination. Traffic was light.

Suddenly, Alexander Grishin sent his car spurting forwards. Apple speeded up only slightly, letting the gap grow. He didn't know if the Russian was aware of his presence, but if not, he wasn't going to advertise it.

The Rover made a sharp right turn. Apple thought it had gone onto another road. Nearing that point, however, he saw that the car had been driven onto the grass and through a break in the palings.

Apple followed.

Now he was tense, worried. While it was unlikely that Grishin would have tried anything with Bill Burton in busy streets, here anything was possible.

Its lights bouncing, the Rover went between the large, well-spaced trees. There was nothing ahead but darkness, which increased as the Russian put his headlights on low.

Apple made his decision. It might blow Bill Burton's game, which in turn could very easily put an end to the undercover career of Appleton Porter. But it might also save Bill's life.

Intent on interception, Apple changed gear and slammed his foot to the floor. The Honda sped forwards. He had a vague hope that Grishin would take this chase car as belonging to the park authority; that he would think he was in minor trouble for leaving the road.

When Apple was twenty feet from the lead car, it swung away to circle a tree. Apple braked. He skidded on the dew-wet grass. Steering his way out, he turned in pursuit—and saw another car among the trees.

Seen only as headlights, the car was approaching at speed from the road where other traffic was passing peacefully. Apple wondered if the new arrival could be what he hoped to be taken for himself.

The Rover swerved again. Ready this time, Apple made the same arc without going out of control. As he did so, his lights flashed across the newcomer. It was the Daimler.

So, Apple thought, gripping his nerves, Kate's tactic hadn't fooled the Hammer and Sickle for long. It was going to be interesting to see what they were up to.

The Rover, speeding, had made a full circle. Now, it was behind Apple, right behind, some ten feet back. That distance was swiftly reduced.

Motor roaring, the Rover slammed into the back of Apple's car.

It jerked forwards. Apple, recovering from the snap of his head and his surprise, sent the Honda racing ahead, then began to circle a tree as a delayer.

The Daimler was coming straight at him.

Cutting his steering wheel violently and severely, Apple made his circle smaller. He brushed by the tree and then saw that the Rover was making a frontal attack.

The following one minute, which seemed like thirty, was for Apple similar to a surrealistic dream. Headlights swept in every direction, engines roared and tyres squealed as the three cars described circles, made charges and went into skids, mostly staying at close range.

Apple had no plan in his head. The sole thought that came was to wonder how dangerous the situation would have to be before Bill Burton judged it time to interfere, thereby cracking his cover.

Arms aching, Apple once again gave his steering wheel a furious spinning. The Honda went into a slide. Apple let it go, and let it slow to its own halt.

Glancing around, dizzy with all the manic action, he saw the Daimler angling towards him at one side, the Rover making straight for him at the other. Both cars were racing.

Apple waited until the lights were dazzlingly close. He shot his car ahead with a leap. He looked back. He winced as the Daimler and Grishin's car met obliquely with a violent crash.

Apple turned back to face front just in time to see the tree he ran into.

CHAPTER 5

What Apple saw next was a black mountain. It rose to a smoothly rounded peak right in front of his eyes, seeming close enough to touch. The sky above it was shiny green.

Apple lowered his eyelids. He sought reassurance by telling himself that he had been in an accident, had been knocked unconscious and was therefore bound to see things oddly for a while—if, in fact, he was actually awake yet.

Eyes open again, Apple still found his vision filled by a black mountain against a glistening green sky. But by looking at both carefully he realised that the peak was the ten-gallon hat, lying on his chest, and that the background was a painted ceiling.

A dull ache throbbed in his forehead. He put a hand there while sitting up. His palm fitted snugly over a lump the size of half an egg. Steering-wheel damage, he noted idly, looking around.

He was on an iron cot with a blanket over the thin mattress. Walls matched ceiling, floor was bare boards. One small window had bars on the other side of the glass. The door struck an odd note here in that it had a regulation handle and no Judas-hole.

Apple got up. He felt fine apart from the ache in his brow. Two steps took him to the door. He tried the handle. It turned. He pulled, and the door opened.

Cautiously, Apple leaned out. More of the shiny green

paint covered a passage that ran in both directions, ending in T-junctions. There was a faint sound of voices.

Retreating, Apple closed the door. Four strides took him to the window. He looked out into a dimly lit yard. There, a man in uniform was leaning boredly on the side of a Black Maria.

Apple accepted that he was in nothing more strange than an English police station. He sagged, part through relief, part out of sadness.

Apple was feeling in a pocket of his denim jacket for cigarettes when the door opened. Bill Burton came in, carrying a tin mug. He said cheerfully, "You're alive, eh? That's good. Here's some tea, hot and sweet as the book prescribes for those in shock or possibly so."

"I'm not in shock, Bill. Just bewildered."

"Aren't we all?"

"I must've been out for hours."

Burton said, "About thirteen minutes. Drink up."

"Yes, sir," Apple said. He took the mug, sat on the cot and began to sip.

"The police surgeon had a look at you. There's nothing wrong apart from that whack on the napper."

"And you?"

"Not a scratch," Bill Burton said, leaning on the wall. "I came out best of all."

"So what's the next step?"

"Isn't one, old son. Your mission, as they say, is concluded. But that's all I know about it so don't throw questions at me."

"Okay," Apple said.

"I've got plenty I'd like to throw at you, but I'm not going to bother."

"I, not unusually, have no answers."

"Old Angus'll fill you in."

"He's here?"

Bill Burton asked, "Angus? And risk being offered police station tea?"

"Maybe I am in shock after all."

"Get that tea down. I'm taking you to see your friend and mine when you've finished."

Apple took a long drink. He said, "Only thirteen minutes. Things've been happening fast."

"They have," Burton said. "But someone turned up to handle the foreign end while I took care of one unwieldy cowboy."

"Thanks, Bill."

"All part of the service."

"That someone," Apple said. "It must've been Kate."

"Who?" Bill Burton asked. His features were abruptly devoid of expression. It was the standard spook face for "Don't tell me, I don't want to know."

"I asked if it was a man with a beard."

"No. You won't have seen this guy around. He's a genius at blending."

Apple wondered if Kate would be all right. He decided yes, with only one person to handle, so long as he wasn't armed. He asked, "How about those other three in our game of Dodg'em cars? Are they all right?"

"That I can tell you, I suppose," Bill Burton said. "The couple have superficial cuts. That other man has a badly fractured leg. He's going to be in traction for months. It's my guess they'll ship him back to wherever he comes from."

So that's why the mission was over, Apple thought. At least he hadn't been pulled out.

He said, "I lost a gun somewhere. Could that other man have taken it from me while I was out?"

"With that leg? It's not likely. Anyway, all he had on him equipmentwise was a small tape recorder. I hope that's not yours."

"No, it isn't."

"I've got it now. I might hear something interesting."

Only an interview between you and Alexander Grishin, Apple mused. Only the fact of knowing this kept him from being embarrassed for having taken the recorder for a pistol.

He said, "Come to think of it, I left my gun in another car."

"Drink up, old son. It's bad policy to keep God waiting."

The place was a few minutes' drive away in Notting Hill Gate. Apple had been to the safe house before. Like all the others in the quiet street, it was detached, small and diffident. The double line of miniature poplars between gate and front door, playing at grandness, was the sole anomaly; one which, however, tended to make the passer-by snub the place for its presumption.

Dropped off out front by Bill Burton, Apple squeaked open the gate and went to the front door. It was opened in answer to his ring by a man who said, "Bloody good job you didn't go and get killed."

"Thank you."

"I mean, where the hell would we get a coffin long enough?"

"Your wit," Apple said, "is as devastating as always."

"Ta," the man said. He was small, middle-aged and wiry, wearing blue coveralls and dirty white running shoes. Known as Albert, he served Angus Watkin in a variety of roles from valet to bodyguard.

He said, "Duck and enter."

Apple went in, trying to hide the Stetson behind his back. But it was seen by Albert, who chuckled, "You're a fair treat for me old eyes tonight."

That Apple kept his reply to a grunt, rather than lashing back, was simply due to his respect for the older man's brilliance at unarmed fighting. Stung, he might give a demonstration.

"Room at the end," Albert said, all humour gone.

Apple went along a short passage. He raised his hand to knock on the door, but before he could, a voice from the other side called, "Come in, Porter."

First blood to Watkin, Apple thought, going through. That bit of business was effective, even though his footsteps on the linoleum had given the cue.

Angus Watkin sat in an armchair in the small den, which smelt faintly of dampness. The emanation that came from Watkin was one of disapproval. This was heightened by the fact that at his elbow was a tray of tea things, already used: the visitor was not going to be offered the ritual cup of tea.

"Do sit down, Porter," Angus Watkin said, as if Apple had been standing there for half an hour.

"Yes, sir." He sat, taking the armchair opposite his Control, who looked him over carefully, starting upwards from the big-heel boots, hovering about the hat on his lap and finishing on his damaged face.

At last, as if tiredly, he said, "Quite."

"Sir?"

"Nothing, Porter, nothing. I've had a short day."

"Yes, sir."

"However, I have other fish to fry, as the coarse say. Therefore I suggest we get to the nub."

"I agree, sir."

"Much obliged," Angus Watkin said. He put his fingertips together, delicately, as though they were afraid of each other. "The mission is over, Porter. Agent Kate has also been informed of that. You will please forget that she exists."

"She's all right?"

"Perfectly," Watkin said. "Now, I shall tell you what's

been going on, and then you will tell me what you thought you were doing tonight. Yes?"

"Yes, sir."

"To begin with, then, the man you know as Alexander Grishin. That is not his real name."

Even though it came as no particular surprise that the Russian would have a different name while abroad, Apple toadied by blinking with fascination.

His chief said, "I do not know, I confess, the name he was born with. He has since had several, all of which I do know. But they are quite meaningless. The point here is, the man you have been following has the sobriquet of Colonel Moscow."

This time, Apple *was* surprised. More, he was astounded. So much so that he responded as though he were in a trance, gaping without a movement anywhere on his body.

Being by necessity of a retiring nature, espionage people rarely ever join the ranks of the celebrated—except when exposed as turncoats. Even within the trade itself, the spies who become names to the rank and file could (as an MI5 wag put it) be counted on the fingers lying on the floor of one small cellar.

Colonel Moscow was countable. He had been an operative with the Komitet Gosudarstvennoi Bezopasnosti since the establishment of the organization under that name—KGB for short (on March 14, 1954, Apple recalled automatically)—and had swiftly risen to being one of its stars. His coups were legend. As Olivier was to acting, Churchill to politics and Renoir to art, so was Colonel Moscow to espionage.

It was not, therefore, the name alone that impressed tyro Appleton Porter, but also the fact that said tyro had been dallying with a spymaster.

Which now made Apple realise yet another awesome factor: he had been considered by Angus Watkin to be a good enough agent to be put into the field against the legendary Colonel Moscow.

Apple quickly changed from gape to preen. He sat up straighter, frowned keenly, hustled his Stetson to a side table, folded his arms like a daring young man between swings on the flying trapeze.

Watkin said, "The name is familiar to you, I imagine."

Apple gave the short, sharp nod of a pro. "It is indeed." His Control, he mused, wasn't a bad old stick really.

"We shall, however, continue to call him Grishin. He thinks he is unrecognised in his menial role, which suits me fine."

"But you have known all along, sir, of course."

"Of course," Angus Watkin said. "Known furthermore that he had several irons in the fire here. I let him keep them, for knowledge is security, while trying to feed him some of my own people as contacts."

"One of whom," Apple said in a cool tone, almost with condescension, "was a certain agent with a scar." Unfolding his arms, he tapped his fingertips together.

"That," Watkin said, "was a closing-stage touch, to keep Grishin from thinking I wanted to get rid of him. I hoped he would suspect that agent of being a double."

Apple lied grandly, "I see."

"The point is that Grishin, being rather clever, was probably running strong contacts while happily letting me be aware of the weak ones. I didn't know but suspected, and so, having exhausted all methods of trying to find out, I decided that Grishin had to go."

Apple, honestly: "I see, sir."

"The usual method is to have the unwanted person expelled for extramural activities. But we know what happens then, don't we, Porter?"

"The Russians retaliate by expelling some of our Moscow embassy staff, at a ratio of perhaps two to one."

"Precisely," Angus Watkin said. "Which could be awkward in the extreme just now, and for some time to come. I have people in Moscow who are involved in important doings. They could be among the expelled."

"Tricky situation," Apple allowed, one equal to another.

"The method from this end would also give away that I know the true identity of Alexander Grishin, which I would rather not have happen."

"Certainly not."

Watkin tapped his forefingers together. "The problem was, how to get Grishin to leave of his own accord. I concluded finally that the best way was to make him believe that he had come to the attention of the Special Branch. That he was being watched constantly. And that there was a danger of all his contacts being blown."

Apple narrowed one eye. "Excellent."

"Therefore," his chief said, "I sent you and agent Kate in to do the watching."

Apple's feelings paused.

As those last words of Watkin's were digested, the pause ended and the decline in spirit began. His steeple of fingers sagged, so that it slowly became a clasp. The grip tightened. His stomach did the same.

Apple saw the bald, dreary truth.

He had been used in this mission not because of his ability, but because of his amateurishness. He had also been used, of course, on account of his noticeable height, in which he had been twinned with an agent of similar style. He had been used because Watkin had expected him to make a mess of the I-spying and so leave the mark in no doubt whatever that he was under observation by non-Upstairs people. He had been used, period.

Angus Watkin said, "You had orders, Porter, to stay clear. This evening you seemed to have ignored that. Perhaps you would be kind enough to explain."

Apple sighed.

"What was that, Porter?"

"I'll gladly explain," Apple said. He was pleased to note that his voice sounded steady, that it betrayed none of his disappointment and anger.

He went on: "At the start of the mission, I quickly realised that it wasn't what it appeared. To begin with, there was the way I was contacted, so urgently, and next all that unnecessary play between agent Kate and myself at Euston Station. I imagine that you assumed, because of my supposed romantic view of the spy game, that I would take it all as real, not look behind the stage dressing. It was clever of you, sir."

"I know. But do continue."

"I also soon realised that Alexander Grishin was no mere menial," Apple lied. "I heard his excellent English, and Kate found a cigarette of his which I knew to be available only to Russia's top people. But I did not, admittedly, guess that he could be anyone as celebrated as Colonel Moscow."

"Of course not."

"I fathomed the strategy of Upstairs," Apple said, shrewdly by-passing his Control, "and decided that it was a shade too obvious to work. Without saying anything to Kate, I formed a plan of my own. All it needed for success was ruthlessness, of which I have a sufficient amount."

"You, Porter?"

"I, sir. I am not, naturally, the same man I was when my dossier was drawn up. That was quite some time ago."

"Don't lose the thread, pray."

Apple, more in charge of his anger now, said, "While waiting for the right moment to do the physical damage that would eliminate Grishin from the game, agent Kate and I operated in a variety of disguises, one of which you see me in here. Kate accepted it as standard procedure.

Alexander Grishin, I'm pleased to say, was never once aware of his shadows."

Angus Watkin looked to be on the verge of going to sleep, which, as Apple knew, meant he was either furious or acutely alert. He asked, "Is there much more of this preamble, Porter?"

Doing a Watkin, pretending he hadn't heard, Apple said, "Tonight I got my opportunity. We saw Grishin and another man leave a hotel and drive off. We followed, using two cars. Following us were Grishin's bodyguards. Kate cleverly managed to draw them off, leaving me free to deal with Grishin. He went off onto the grass in Hyde Park and I was about to ram him when the Hammer and Sickle caught up, so I used their car as I had been taught in Driving 5 at Damian House."

Sighing, Angus Watkin asked, "And Grishin's passenger?"

"Luckily, I caught sight of him in the headlights during the skirmish. I was able to arrange for the collision to occur on the driver's side of the car."

Angus Watkin closed his eyes. Apple rose from the chair. He picked up his hat and put it on at a jaunty angle. He said, bringing Watkin's eyes open, "Alexander Grishin, in my trained opinion, has a badly fractured leg that's going to need months of traction and care. It's my guess they'll ship him back to Moscow at once."

Apple turned away. "But I mustn't take up any more of your time, sir. Good night."

Firmly ignoring Albert's parting shot and the fact that there were a couple of loose ends lying around, Apple left the house. He walked quickly. It was a damp night.

The remains of Apple's anger swiftly crumbled away. He began to see the plusses, starting with the fact that he had just won an interview with Angus bloody Watkin.

He *had* succeeded in accomplishing the mission's goal.

He *had* kept Alexander Grishin in ignorance of being tailed. He *had* survived tests to his body and his nerve. He *had* locked horns with the great Colonel Moscow. He *had* met a wonderful girl.

His spirits up, Apple began to walk faster. Soon he was on Queensway with its lights and babble of tongues. Many business places were still open, as well as all the snack joints and restaurants.

Beside a newspaper stand Apple found a telephone box. He dented his hat going in, looked coldly at the browsers who had stopped reading newspapers, fed the slot and dialled. He had just footed the door ajar when Kate answered.

They started to talk at the same time. Apple ended it by asking, "What happened to you?"

"Those two behind soon tumbled. They peeled off. I tried to pick up again but I got nowhere. Then an agent, one I know, drove up beside me and said it was all over."

"Yes, the caper's finished."

"Why? What happened? I'm dying to know."

"I can't talk here," Apple said. "If we could meet. Now. Say, in that Soho restaurant."

"If the mission's over, we ought not to meet," Kate said. "I'll be there in thirty minutes."

Apple left the telephone box, raised his hat to the non-readers and walked on. He mused that thirty minutes would give him just enough time to go home, get shut of the Stetson and quickly change into comfortable foot-wear.

Also, while he was there and as it was a damp night, he might as well put on a coat. Any kind of coat would do. The first coat that came to hand. It was wise to wear a coat in damp weather. They were sensible things, coats.

A minute later, Apple found that he had stopped walking. He was gazing at a man and woman, bronzely tanned, who were strolling along a palm-fringed beach.

The picture, he noted, was in the window of a travel agency.

Apple was getting ideas. Most were unoriginal; they had been around since Eden and the first apple. But the paramount notion was novel, at least insofar as Apple had never had it before during his love life.

Supposing, he thought, when the meal in Soho was over, and they were mellow with food, wine and affection; supposing he were to casually drop an air ticket on the table, name the exotic destination and say a quiet but masterly "The plane takes off at ten tomorrow morning. We will be on it."

Apple hesitated. He had his credit card with him and the agency was open. It wouldn't hurt to go in and ask. But, if he did make bookings and did try the approach on Kate, what would her reaction be? Would he get a warm hello or a decisive good-bye?

Apple thought about it.

The restaurant, small and intimate, was Tuesday quiet, three quarters of the tables empty. Apple was able to choose a place at the side, where he could sit with his back to the wall in true spook fashion. Which he did, after declining to let the waiter help him off with his trench coat.

The second candle that Apple asked for had been brought and lit when Kate came in. She looked stunning in a blue knitted dress with cardigan to match.

When they were both sitting, greetings over, Kate said, "All right, Basil, tell me the works. Or anyway, as much as the rules allow."

Bearing need-to-know in mind, even though it irked him to have to do so, Apple left out the Hammer and Sickle and Grishin's famous nickname in relating the scene in Hyde Park. He said he had rammed the Rover, pointing to his lump as evidence.

Kate asked, "You saved the Brit?"

Apple said nonchalantly, "He's unharmed, yes, though we can't be sure of Grishin's intentions. He, by the way, is a little mangled. He's out of the game."

"And we didn't find out how he was playing it."

"That's for Upstairs to worry about now," Apple said. "Angus and I had a little chat afterwards on that score." He leaned forwards. "I did not, incidentally, mention anything about the hotel room."

Kate said, "A nod is as good as a wink."

The waiter came to get their orders. Kate handed him her menu: "Steak, please. Also a salad—no onions."

Apple smiled. "I'll have the same. And you may bring a red of good family. The selection I leave to you." The last he said as if he knew all about wines and wanted to test the waiter's knowledge.

Alone again, Apple and Kate lit cigarettes. Kate said she smoked only on special occasions.

"And this is one?"

"Yes, Basil."

"End of mission, you mean?"

Giving her quiet smile, Kate said, "No, end of career. The mission was my last."

"Spooks're always saying that. I've said it myself more than once."

"In my case, Basil, it's a little different. I'll let you in on a secret, shall I?"

"If you feel you can."

"I do," Kate said. "It's just that not only was the caper my last, it was also my first."

"It was your . . . ?"

She nodded. "I'd never been out in the field before. I'm a code freak normally. I had all the basic training, of course, but I'd never used it. I was as raw as an east wind."

"You were . . . ?"

"Tonight, I'm afraid, I chickened out after I learned that our Alex had a gun. That's why I let you do the fore bit. I didn't want an armed man behind me. Sorry about that."

Apple shrugged.

"But you obviously have survived the gun, Basil."

After a pause, Apple shrugged again.

The matter was held there by the waiter's arrival with a bottle. The wine ritual, which Apple usually went through meekly though considering it fatuous, he was largely unaware of. He was seeing in retrospect all the pointers/clues to Kate's amateur status.

Often she had asked his opinion on tactics, not, as he'd thought, out of kindness, but because she didn't know. She had overused spookspeak. At Earl's Court she had without question taken the less important part as fore-twin. Calling Angus Watkin "Mr." was real, not born of sarcasm. When she lost Grishin's cab that time, she didn't ditch the Fiesta and follow in some other way. Her "Routine 7" at the telephone box in the bird sanctuary had been the kind of thing no pro would try—which is precisely why it had worked, Grishin suspecting nothing.

Tonight the amateur had begun to come through strongly: her overplaying at the reception desk, her suggestion that Apple ask the clerk for a tool, her interest in the gift bouquet. Undressing to save the occasion, that had been feminine instinct.

Apple became aware that the waiter had gone and that Kate had a glass raised. He lifted his own and said, "You were brilliant."

"I hardly dare believe that, but I'll try," Kate said. "Here's to us."

"To us."

They sipped. Putting her glass down, Kate sagged

back in the chair and let her arms flop. She smiled broadly, showing deep dimples.

"What a relief," she said. "How fab that I can now be myself and stop acting the cool, calculating agent. Wow." She laughed.

Apple was delighted with the animation in Kate's face. He watched avidly as she talked about how worried she had been during the operation and about the mistakes she had made or nearly made. She was still talking when the food arrived.

They ate busily and, for a while, in silence. Waving his fork, Apple asked what made her think that Upstairs wouldn't want to use her again.

"Oh, I didn't mean that when I told you this was my last caper," Kate said. "The thing is, I'm quitting."

"Retiring?"

"Yes. Leaving the Service altogether, codes included. It's all settled."

"It is?"

"Very definitely."

Apple chewed, swallowed. "That's good," he said. "We'll be able to see each other from now on without breaking any regulations."

Kate shook her head with blinks of regret. "Sorry."

Apple asked, "Eh?"

They both looked aside as the waiter came. "A gentleman left this for you, sir," he said. He put down a newsprint-wrapped package the size of a hefty sandwich.

He left, and Apple asked again, "Eh?"

"The main reason I'm quitting the Service," Kate said, "is because I'm getting married."

Apple subsided slowly. "Oh."

"I know that sounds terribly old-fashioned, and frankly I'd rather be a working wife, but it so happens that my boy friend is insanely jealous."

Apple nodded glumly. "I see."

"Other from that, he's perfect," Kate said, becoming enthusiastic. She went on to list all Herbert's qualities, ending with a physical description. "And he has this gorgeous full, dark beard."

"Ah," Apple said.

"So, Basil, much as I like you and enjoy your company, I'm afraid it wouldn't be wise for us to meet again."

He fingered the bruise on his jaw. "You're quite right."

"Still," Kate said brightly, "we can enjoy this, can't we? The steak is delicious."

Apple had lost his appetite. Depressed, he sipped the wine. After a moment Kate said, "Please note that I'm not showing any curiosity about that package."

Idly, Apple picked it up and stripped off the newsprint. Revealed was an inner wrapping of brown paper and a white envelope. The latter bore the letters FYEO.

Kate put down her knife and fork. "I'm just about finished anyway," she said. "Carry on and feed your eyes only while I go to powder my nose." She had got up and moved away before Apple could give even a token rise. He watched her swaying form with deep regret.

Opening the envelope, Apple brought out a piece of paper. The message typed on it said, "You left the house before I had a chance to give you this money. Your vehicle is in Service garage number 2."

Apple began to shake his head slowly. That was surprise. Ending the shake, he drew his head backwards. That was disbelief. He started to give long nods. That was acceptance. He smiled. That was relief, amusement and esteem.

Apple didn't mind being last-worded by Angus Watkin this way, nor did he care about the reprimand for fraternisation implied by the ransom money being returned here rather than to his home. He was happy to know that Ethel was safe, diverted by the irony of it all and impressed with his Control's machinations:

Having had Ethel seized and put in an Upstairs garage, all Watkin need do when, to further other designs, he wanted Alexander Grishin unmolested, was arrange to have his green underling go to a rendezvous with the supposed carnappers. The even greener twin would present few problems.

His spirits rising, Apple stuffed the package of money into a pocket of his trench coat. He gave Angus Watkin full marks, not least for being aware of Appleton Porter's devotion to his car.

Apple held the note over a candle. He watched the flames with warm, gleaming eyes. The warped black remains he was crumbling into the ashtray when Kate came back.

He began to get up, but sat again when she said, "Please stay where you are. In fact, don't move. I want to remember you like this. Always."

Remaining on her feet beside the table, Kate continued, "I'm leaving now, Basil, but before I go I want you to know that it's been a privilege. I feel honoured. I count myself lucky that I was able to work with a real pro on my one and only mission. Thank you."

"Well . . ."

Kate held up a hand. "No, you don't have to say anything. I realise that mostly you can't, just as I realise there was more to this operation than there appeared. Need-to-know kept me out of some of it, such as your long absence this evening from our room at the hotel. That's quite as it should be."

Apple said, "Mmm."

"Mr. Watkin told me not to mention this," Kate said, "because you tend to be prickly on the subject—out of modesty. But you're a star operator. You've been on doz- **N52** ens of missions. You know the trade backwards. In fact, your father was also in the Service."

"Ah," Apple said.

Smiling quietly, Kate let her eyes rove. She took in the brow lump, the cut eyebrow, the bruised jaw, the trench coat, the black mess in the ashtray.

"Another thing I shouldn't mention," she said, "but I can't help playing spy, is the air ticket in your jacket pocket. I glimpsed it earlier, when you got out cigarettes. That means you're off on another mission straight away, doesn't it, Basil?"

Apple nodded. "Tomorrow."

"I know it's breaking the rules to ask this, but where're you going?"

Apple admitted, "Switzerland."

Kate sighed. She began to back away. "I'll never forget you," she said. "Never." Turning, she walked to the exit. After a final look back, she went out.

Apple, his eyes dreamy, sat on. He sat on for quite a long time, not moving.

ABOUT THE AUTHOR

Marc Lovell is the author of five previous Appleton Porter novels, including *Apple to the Core, Apple Spy in the Sky* and *Spy on the Run,* as well as many others, including *Hand over Mind* and *A Voice from the Living.* Mr. Lovell has lived on the island of Majorca for the last twenty years.